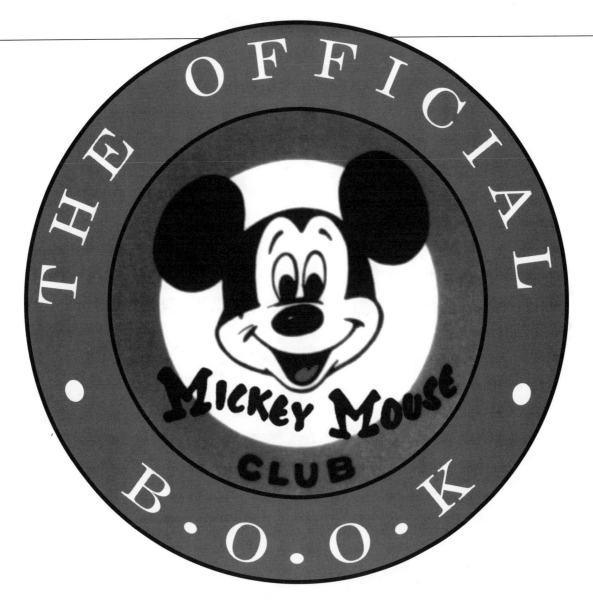

THE OFFICIAL
MICKEY MOUSE CLUB
B·O·O·K

BY LORRAINE SANTOLI

HYPERION

NEW YORK

To my mother, father, and brother Robert,
the three most important people in my life

Library of Congress Cataloging-in-Publication Data

Santoli, Lorraine
    The official Mickey Mouse Club book / by Lorraine Santoli. — 1st ed.
        p. cm.
    Includes index.
    ISBN 0-7868-8042-2
    1. Mickey Mouse Club (television program)   I. Title.
PN1992.77.M53S36   1995
791.45'72—dc20   94-38707
                                                         First Edition

10 9 8 7 6 5 4 3 2 1

Design/production by Robert Bull Design

CONTENTS

ACKNOWLEDGMENTS

The author would like to take this opportunity to thank the people whose assistance was invaluable to the development of this book: Dave Smith, Robert Tieman, and Becky Cline of The Walt Disney Archives, the gatekeepers of Disney history; Steve Rogers and Ed Squair of the Disney Photo Library; Paula Sigman of The Walt Disney Collectors Society; Patty Romanowski, a wonderful writer who provided me the organizational key to write this book; Bob Miller, publisher and vice-president of Hyperion, for his belief that I could do it; Lauren Marino, my editor; and, last and most important, so many of the original Mouseketeers, whose friendships I treasure.

FOREWORD
by
ANNETTE FUNICELLO

I REMEMBER THAT FIRST DAY at the Disney Studio was very weird. We saw these hats that we had to wear, with big black ears, and shirts with our names across the chest. What is a Mouseketeer? What is a "Mickey Mouse Club"? What are we all going to be doing? Well, it didn't take long before we were well into the routine of working on what was to become a classic program in the history of children's television, although we didn't know it at the time.

For me, the years I spent on "The Mickey Mouse Club" show were some of the best of my life. Not only am I grateful that it did so much to bring me out of my shell (I was so shy!), but it enabled me to meet so many great people and visit so many fantastic places that I never would have done on my own. I also got a great education at the studio and formed special friendships with the other Mouseketeers, many of whom are still my closest friends. Of course, one of the best things about "The Mickey Mouse Club" was that I got to know Walt Disney. He meant so much to me.

For the kids at home watching the show, they got to be entertained, educated, and taught many of life's lessons in a most enjoyable way. Maybe that's why even now, forty years later, memories of "The Mickey Mouse Club" still bring a smile to people's faces.

When people stop me today, wherever I am, and say, "Where are your ears?" I say, "Right here," pointing to my own ears. "No," they say, "the other ears." And I tell them they're bronzed and sitting in my living room. I had them bronzed so every time I pass by, I'd be reminded of wonderful memories. I owe everything to those ears and feel so lucky to have been one of the chosen few who can call themselves original Mouseketeers.

Annette Funicello

INTRODUCTION

*It's my personal opinion that "The Mickey Mouse
Club" will revolutionize daytime television. Not only
will it be a most successful children's program, but a
tremendous family show also.*

— ROBERT E. KINTNER, President, ABC-TV,
September 26, 1955

IT WAS 5 P.M. ON MONDAY, OCTOBER 3, 1955. Characteristic
of the era, most moms were in the kitchen preparing dinner while
dad was leaving his workplace heading home. A sizable segment of
America's children were stationed in front of a relatively new
entertainment phenomenon — a television set — and tuned in to
the ABC Television Network. Under the black-and-white image of
an animated billboard illuminated by klieg lights, an announcer
with a voice that millions of kids would soon become accustomed
to ushered in a show that was to leave its mark on a generation
of baby boomers: "Walt Disney and Mickey Mouse present 'The
Mickey Mouse Club.'"

As the circular "Mickey Mouse Club" logo appeared on the screen, three animated Mickey Mouse fanfare trumpeters commenced the musical introduction, an anthem a generation would come to know well:

Rrr-um-pa pum-pa-pum
RRR-UM-PA PUM-PA-PUM

Who's the leader of the club
That's made for you and me?
M-I-C, K-E-Y, M-O-U-S-E.
Hey there, hi there, ho there
You're as welcome as can be,
M-I-C, K-E-Y, M-O-U-S-E.
Mickey Mouse! Donald Duck!
Mickey Mouse! Donald Duck!
Forever let us hold our banner high,
High, High, High!
Come along and sing a song
And join the jamboree,
M-I-C, K-E-Y, M-O-U-S-E
Yay, Mickey!
Yay, Mickey!
Yay, Mickey Mouse Club!

    The Disney characters who marched through the opening scene were familiar figures — Donald Duck, Goofy, Dumbo, Jiminy Cricket, the Three Little Pigs, Daisy Duck, and Minnie Mouse. They had appeared in cartoons, animated films, in books, on records, and imprinted on a great variety of Disney merchandise. They had become household names.

    Then Mickey himself appeared, playing the piano. Decked out in his Monday attire of striped jacket, straw hat, and cane, he welcomed the viewing audience with a cheery "Hi, Mouseketeers!" "Hi, Mickey!" responded a group of unseen children as we at home joined in. "Big doings this

week," Mickey promised. "Adventure, fun, music, cartoons, news. Everybody ready?" "Ready!" we eagerly answered. "Then on with the show!" We were about to step into television history.

Following World War II, some 73,000,000 babies were born in America, creating the largest population explosion in our history. Representing a cross-section of American society, boomers were reared during a period of economic growth and technological advances. It was an era that spurred the growth of mass media — music, film, radio, theater, and, of course, television.

Viewed through the eyes of a child, which I was, it was not a time of the Cold War and bomb shelters or racial confrontations and the anti-Communist hysteria of the McCarthy hearings. Rather, it was a great time — innocent and full of the notion that it was a beautiful and uncomplicated world. There would be enough time to deal with the realities of life in the decades to come.

With an original four-year run, along with numerous years in syndication, "The Mickey Mouse Club" ultimately became a universal children's viewing habit. However, it was not Walt Disney's first foray into sponsoring a Mickey Mouse Club.

In September 1929, Harry W. Woodin, manager of the Fox Dome Theater in Ocean Park, California, presented Walt Disney with the idea of a theater-sponsored club that would be associated with Mickey Mouse. Walt's new character made his debut on November 18, 1928, at the Colony Theater in New York City, in the world's first fully synchronized sound cartoon, "Steamboat Willie," from which Mickey emerged as a major screen star. With the complete cooperation of the Disney studio, Woodin organized the first Mickey Mouse Club.

In light of Mickey's huge success, it was amazing that he had been born only a year earlier, as legend has it, in the imagination of Walt Disney on a train ride from New York to Los Angeles. Walt was returning with his wife from a business meeting at which his cartoon creation Oswald the Lucky Rabbit had been wrested from him by his financial backers.

Only twenty-six years old at the time and with an active cartoon studio in Hollywood, Walt had gone east to arrange for a new contract and more money to improve the quality of his Oswald pictures. The moneymen declined, and since the character was copyrighted under their name, they took control of it.

"...so I was all alone and had nothing," Walt recalled in a Disney Studio bio. "Mrs. Disney and I were coming back from New York on the train and I had to have something....I couldn't tell them I'd lost Oswald...so, I had this mouse in the back of my head...because a mouse is sort of a sympathetic character in spite of the fact that everybody's frightened of a mouse...including myself."

Walt spent the return train ride conjuring up a little mouse in red velvet pants and named him Mortimer, but by the time the train screeched into the terminal station in Los Angeles, the new dream mouse had been rechristened. Walt's wife, Lillian, thought the name Mortimer was too pompous and suggested Mickey. A star was born.

Soon after Mickey's debut, the Disney Studio entered an era of prosperity that became known as Mickey's Golden Age, a decade in which the studio produced the greatest number of Mickey Mouse cartoons. It was the perfect time to launch the theater-based Mickey Mouse clubs.

As described in *Disneyana: Walt Disney Collectibles*, by Cecil Munsey, the two primary purposes of the club were: (1) to provide an easily arranged and inexpensive method of getting and holding the patronage of youngsters; and (2) through inspirational, patriotic, and character-building activities

Mickey seeks members for the first Mickey Mouse Club.

OFFICIAL BULLETIN
—of the—
MICKEY MOUSE CLUB

L. A. BENEDICT, General Manager
HAM BEALL, Editor   **R. M. FINCH,** Managing Editor
Address All Communications to
Walt Disney Studios, 2719 Hyperion Ave., Hollywood

VOL. II, No. 1   JANUARY 1, 1932

START A MEMBERSHIP DRIVE!

MICKEY APPEARS IN RECORD SHOW

Mickey Mouse was the featured cartoon on what is believed to be the world's record endurance show recently staged at Lakemba, Australia. Eight features were presented on the bill, which ran from 10:30 in the morning until 5:30 o'clock in the afternoon for one admission.

Publicity matter invited patrons to "Come early—Bring your lunch—Stop all day—No extra charge." The admission price was a quarter with half price for the children. And the bill was staged on a holiday at that!

Airplane Gifts

Proof that Young America is still air-minded is given by the stimulation of attendance at the Fox Egyptian Mickey Mouse Club in Long Beach, California, through the giving away of Thunderbird monoplanes, arranged through the cooperation of 22 Long Beach merchants. One plane is being given away each Saturday for a 10 weeks' period.

The manager has found the giving away of the miniature aircraft not only stimulates the attendance of regular members of the club, but attracts many other youngsters to sign up for membership.

MICKEY MOUSE'S MUSINGS

• • •

The glorious holidays are over and Yours Truly with Minnie and the rest of our company have buckled down to work again, with a firm resolve to give you the finest sound cartoons possible in 1932.

I note with great pleasure that Liberty Weekly has put the Mickey Mouse cartoons at the head of its list of 1931 achievements in short subjects, but I assure you that it hasn't gone to my head or Walt Disney's and we know we have hard work cut out for us during the coming year.

Again I want to congratulate the managers on the great progress made in building up the Mickey Mouse Clubs to their present top position among juvenile organizations of the kind in the country.

Now Is the Time to Get Busy Enrolling Children To Help Your Box-Office

This issue of the Mickey Mouse Bulletin marks the inauguration of a new volume of the publication and the advent of a new year for the hundreds of Mickey Mouse Clubs throughout the length and breadth of the land.

During the twelve-month past, scores of new Mickey Mouse Clubs have been added to the roster, and indications are that before another new year rolls around, the number will be doubled.

Mickey Mouse Is Winning Fun Film

Mickey Mouse tops the comedy field for both adults and children to judge by the results of a recent poll conducted at the Vilas theatre at Eagle Rock, Wisconsin. He polled more than half the votes.

Second place went to Laurel and Hardy with "Our Gang" a close third. The most popular male star was Richard Dix, while Greta Garbo, despite the legion of imitators, holds her place as first lady of the screen. Robert Montgomery and Joan Crawford tied for second place. The manager conducted the contest in the form of a questionnaire to determine the desires of his audiences. He has arranged to show several "demand pictures."

There is no time like the present to build up your club and put your theatre in a position to cash in at the box-office on the future of this juvenile organization that is sweeping the country.

Put on an active membership drive now! Several of the clubs are already doing it and are being astonished at the results they are achieving. An account of these activities is printed elsewhere in the Bulletin.

It should not be hard for an aggressive manager to realize that right now the children offer the best means of bringing adult patronage to the theatre, when finances in general are at a low ebb and the box-office suffering.

Parents will deny themselves for their children and will strain their budgets to permit the youngsters to attend the theatre, even if they

(Continued on Page Three)

related to the club, to aid children in learning good citizenship, which in turn fostered good will among parents. There were also the unmentioned purposes of making Mickey Mouse cartoons more popular and promoting character merchandise.

In addition to eventually becoming a Disney employee and overseeing clubs across the country, Woodin developed a semi-monthly newsletter called the *Official Bulletin of the Mickey Mouse Club,* which was published on the first and fifteenth of each month and was sent to the theater managers who had established clubs. The first issue was published on April 15, 1930, less than two years after the debut of the cartoon star.

Mickey Mouse Club meetings were held at local theaters at the beginning of matinees, which almost always took place at noon on Saturdays. The theater manager usually had a working arrangement with a number of local merchants who were involved in selling products and services to children. Since the local clubs increased sales, it was not difficult to obtain the merchants' cooperation.

Some of the businesses that participated in Mickey Mouse clubs included: bakeries, which offered a free birthday cake on Saturday for each child who had celebrated a birthday during the previous week; florists, which sent a small bouquet to sick club members; dairies, which offered ice cream prizes; banks, which gave a free savings bank toy to club members; department stores, which gave inexpensive toys to club members to encourage the purchase of more toys; photographers; sporting goods stores; jewelry stores; candy stores; drugstores; and almost any and all neighborhood merchants.

Local Parent-Teacher Associations and schools were often supporters of Mickey Mouse clubs, and club members with high marks in school were given special membership cards. Although membership in the club was free, the children paid to get into the

The *Official Bulletin of the Mickey Mouse Club.*

theaters where the meeting was held. At each such session a club officer began the meeting by reading the creed of the Mickey Mouse Club.

The audience then spoke the Mickey Mouse pledge in unison: "Mickey Mice do not swear, smoke, cheat or lie." Next, the flag was brought on stage and saluted, followed by one verse of "America." Various games were then played, acts presented, stunts shown, and contests held. Finally, the group was led in the Mickey Mouse Club yell:

Handy! Dandy!
Sweet as candy!
Happy kids are we!
Eenie! Ickie!
Minnie! Mickey!
M-O-U-S-E!

The meeting was concluded when the words to The Mickey Mouse Club song "Minnie's Yoo Hoo" were flashed on the screen and everybody sang.

Mickey Mouse "Theme Song"

We're the gang they call little Mickey Mice
And we're always mighty nice
Whether fat or skinny we're the Horse's whinny
Reg'lar little Mickey Mice.

Before 1930 drew to a close, there were hundreds of clubs all over the nation, and in foreign countries as well. At its height, in 1932, the Mickey Mouse Club had over a million members in the United States — or, as a writer in the October 1, 1932, issue of *Motion Picture Herald* put it, the club's "membership approximates that of the Boy Scouts and Girl Scouts of America, combined."

Twenty-three years later, almost to the day, the second version of "The Mickey Mouse Club" made its debut. At its core, it possessed many of the wholesome attributes and virtuous ideals set forth in its previous incarnation, this time personified by Jimmie Dodd, the wholesome adult leader of the club, and a group of talented, clean-cut kids-next-door known as the Mouseketeers.

"The Mickey Mouse Club"'s first-year team of twenty-four mouse-eared kids had, in fact, been introduced via television to the American public three months prior to their show's debut, on July 17, 1955, at the grand opening of the world's first theme park, Disneyland, in Anaheim, California.

Broadcast live on ABC-TV, "Dateline Disneyland" was phenomenally successful in introducing the American public to Walt's

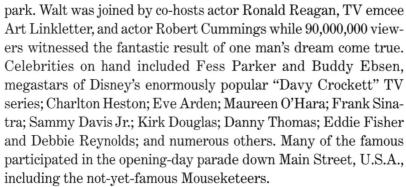

park. Walt was joined by co-hosts actor Ronald Reagan, TV emcee Art Linkletter, and actor Robert Cummings while 90,000,000 viewers witnessed the fantastic result of one man's dream come true. Celebrities on hand included Fess Parker and Buddy Ebsen, megastars of Disney's enormously popular "Davy Crockett" TV series; Charlton Heston; Eve Arden; Maureen O'Hara; Frank Sinatra; Sammy Davis Jr.; Kirk Douglas; Danny Thomas; Eddie Fisher and Debbie Reynolds; and numerous others. Many of the famous participated in the opening-day parade down Main Street, U.S.A., including the not-yet-famous Mouseketeers.

Covering the procession, Art Linkletter, in voice-over as the cameras focused on the parade, described the new Disney stars,

Ronald Reagan, Bob Cummings, and Art Linkletter co-host "Dateline Disneyland," along with Walt Disney.

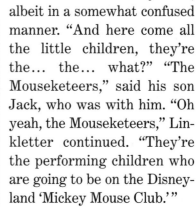

albeit in a somewhat confused manner. "And here come all the little children, they're the... the... what?" "The Mouseketeers," said his son Jack, who was with him. "Oh yeah, the Mouseketeers," Linkletter continued. "They're the performing children who are going to be on the Disneyland 'Mickey Mouse Club.'"

The "performing children" did just that later in the broadcast. With cameras stationed outside the Mickey Mouse Club Theater in Fantasyland, twenty-four young unknowns came rushing through the doorway as Robert Cummings announced, "And now from inside the theater come the Mouseketeers, a group of talented boys and girls who will be on 'The Mickey Mouse Club' this fall, October 3rd, and I guarantee you many a future star will be coming out of this group."

A number of the contingent were attired in western wear and launched into the Talent Round-Up song we would soon become familiar with: "Saddle your pony, here we go down to the talent rodeo. Gather up Susie, Jack and Joe, join the talent round-up." The rest of the kids, wearing their name shirts and mouse ears, sang and jitterbugged to a swing tune, followed by Jimmie Dodd's proclaiming, for the first time, "Mouseketeer roll call, count off now!"

The twenty-four kids and two adult Mouseketeers lined up in front of the camera as each took a turn enthusiastically shouting their name: Bonnie! Bobby! Sharon! Lonnie! Darlene! Don! Doreen! Tommy! Judy! Lee! Dennis! Mary! Paul! Mary! Billie! Mark! Bronson! Mickey! Karen! Cubby! Mike! Nancy! Johnny! Annette! Roy! Jimmie!

I experienced a similar roll call "live" some twenty-five years later when I walked onto Soundstage One at the Walt Disney Studio and became acquainted with the original Mouseketeers for the first time. There they were, all grown up and rehearsing for their 25th reunion television special. As a Disney publicist, I had been

The Mouseketeers get ready for their first public appearance.

given the assignment to take over the publicity reins of the show when the production's initial publicist, Missy Sutton, left the show to go on maternity leave.

Witnessing the rehearsal that afternoon encompassed me in a wave of nostalgia so strong that the two and a half decades that had passed since I was first introduced to "The Mickey Mouse Club" were erased in my mind like so much chalk on a blackboard. I was just seven years old again, watching, singing, and enjoying with my friends the Mouseketeers. How fortunate I felt to be able to share this experience with people I had grown up with, albeit via a TV set. Little did I know that it was to be the beginning of an association with the Mouseketeers that would endure through many shows, special events, and publicity tours.

My personal experience with the Mouseketeers has spanned fifteen years from working with them on shows and publicity at Disneyland, Walt Disney World, and in cities across the United States and around the world. My relationship extends well beyond the boundaries of business; they've become good friends. I guess I've been able to live out a childhood fantasy — only several decades later! Even through job changes at Disney to my present position of Manager, Corporate Special Projects, all queries about the original Mouseketeers ultimately get directed to me.

Over the course of a four-year run (1955–59), thirty-nine original Mouseketeers appeared on the show. While each was talented in their own right, this book will primarily focus on the nine Mouseketeers who worked on the show from day one until the end of the series and who appeared most often on roll call: Sharon Baird, Bobby Burgess, Lonnie Burr, Tommy Cole, Annette Funi-

"Saddle your pony, here we go."

cello, Darlene Gillespie, Cubby O'Brien, Karen Pendleton, and Doreen Tracey.

In the mid-1980s, Mouseketeers Sherry Alberoni (1956–57 season), Bonnie Lynn Fields (1957–58 season), and Don Grady (1957–58 season) also became active participants in Disney shows and special events. In fact, Sherry traveled extensively with Bobby Burgess and myself in celebration of Mickey Mouse's 60th birthday in 1988. The three of us had some unusual experiences.

I remember in Sydney when Bobby, Sherry, and Mickey Mouse appeared live on "Good Morning, Australia," the Aussies' equivalent of our "Good Morning, America." After the show host introduced the threesome, he went on to explain how he was going to pull off a never-before-attempted feat — expose Mickey by removing his head. I was standing just out of camera range as a look of utter shock came over the faces of Bobby and Sherry. Quickly responding to the outrageous contention, Sherry hastily replied, "Take off Mickey's head? Mickey's head doesn't come off — take off *Bobby's* head!" Laughter prevailed — she saved the day.

Then there was the time in San Diego when Bobby and Sherry were to do an interview on a live radio show. We had had lunch at a Mexican restaurant just before the show, and each of them had ordered a margarita — quite unusual since neither drank very often. We left the restaurant and headed for the radio station. I was driving a rental car and Bobby and Sherry were sitting in the back seat. By the time we reached the station, about thirty minutes later, I was faced with having to awaken two dead-asleep, snoring Mouseketeers. No more margaritas before an interview.

Our Washington, D.C., adventure left much to be desired. The day had started out on the wrong foot in California on the way to the airport. Traffic was heavy and our limo driver was inexperienced. The result — we missed the plane that would have gotten us to Washington at about six o'clock in the evening. The next available flight was four hours later. After watching 240 minutes tick away, we were finally aboard and on our way.

Several hours later, as the plane approached Washington, we hit an electrical thunderstorm that illuminated the night sky as I anxiously peered out the window. We ended up being the last plane to land (thank goodness!) that night. However, I had never been to Washington, and had to drive us in a rental car in the pouring rain to our hotel, the Watergate (how aptly named for that evening). We got lost. Very, very, very lost.

Some two hours later, at about midnight, we reached our destination, exhausted. Oh, to get in bed and get some sleep! But it was not to be that simple. When we checked in, we found that the desk clerk had given away our rooms and the hotel was completely booked. Could anything more go wrong? After much disgruntled discussion, the manager relented with a solution — Bobby would get the Presidential Suite and Sherry and I would share a suite/apartment whose residents were out of town.

There have been many fun adventures with many Mouseketeers. After fifteen years of mice-minding, and now through much archival "Mickey Mouse Club" research and interviews both with the core group and with others connected to the original show, I'm thrilled to have had the opportunity to write this book. As one fan told me while I was researching:

"I watched 'The Mickey Mouse Club' every night — planted in front of the TV at 5 p.m. with my ears on ready to sing along with the theme song. Even though it was a TV show, it gave me a sense of belonging."

For me, it still does.

Lorraine Santoli
August 1994

1
THE BEGINNING

*Instead of considering TV a rival, when I
saw it, I said, "I can use that; I want
to be a part of it."*

— WALT DISNEY

AS EARLY AS THE 1930S, WALT DISNEY had allowed Mickey Mouse cartoons to be used in tests of television transmitting equipment. Most Hollywood producers at the time were quite unimpressed by the new medium. In fact, Deak Aylesworth, a well-known radio-film executive at RKO Pictures during this era, dutifully assured Hollywood that it had "nothing to fear from television as a competitive factor."

The New York Times scrutinized "the new development" and reported that motion picture producers remained unworried since radio was "digging in" in Hollywood as protection against the time when television encroached on their territory. Even the Motion Picture Academy, which had engaged in an official study of television's status, came to a happy conclusion. The television picture was too small, costs too high, and patronage meager. But young cartoon producer Walt Disney, who had been closely following the development of the new medium, revealed his visionary thinking when he remarked, "I'm looking to the future, and that includes television."

On Christmas Day, 1950, the first Disney television show — "One Hour in Wonderland," sponsored by the Coca-Cola Company — was aired. As a result of its excellent ratings, Walt produced a similar show during the holiday season the following year, "The Walt Disney Christmas Show," which resulted in a second ratings blockbuster. With the popularity of these shows, Walt received many proposals to produce a regular series of television programs. He had refused all offers and only agreed to annual shows because he could do them on his own terms, which meant, at the time, that there would be a commercial announcement only at the beginning and the ending of the programs.

Despite his reluctance, however, he realized the benefits of having weekly shows to use as a promotional vehicle for his other interests. In keeping with that focus, he had his creative team develop several series ideas.

On October 1, 1953, initial ideas were outlined for four Disney television shows: "The Walt Disney Show," "The True Life Show," "The World of Tomorrow" and "The Mickey Mouse Club." The first sentences of the outline decreed that "any presentation of the Walt Disney name and product must be prefaced by these facts: 1. Good taste in entertainment; 2. Quality production; 3. Broad family audience appeal."

"The Walt Disney Show" was described as an evening show, with Walt Disney himself as master of ceremonies, to be highlighted by the top product from the extensive Disney library of film, plus fascinating behind-the-scenes glimpses from all new Walt Disney features.

"The True Life Show" originated from the "True-Life Adventure" section of Disneyland and showcased the strange and wondrous facts of reality in both human and animal life. Disney's award-winning

"One Hour in Wonderland," Walt Disney's very first television show, starred (from left to right): Kathryn Beaumont, the voice of Alice in the Disney film *Alice in Wonderland;* Charlie McCarthy and famous ventriloquist Edgar Bergen; and child star Bobby Driscoll.

"True-Life Adventure" films would, in part, provide the programming, along with guests that would include famous naturalists, educators, and scientists.

"The World of Tomorrow" combined the history of man's development in the past with man's dreams and hopes for the future, and was also to combine both live action and animation. Subjects proposed to be covered included The History of Aviation, The Story of the Wheel, Facts About Electricity, and The Story of Man.

"The Mickey Mouse Club" was to be a live, five-day-a-week children's show headquartered at Disneyland. The format was described as inspirational and educational through humorous entertainment. The plan stated that each week the setting of the show would be in a different part of the world. The children would be transported by the show's genie magician to spots on the globe interesting to all children.

Regular members of the cast would include a gadget band playing the type of music children like, a comic as master of ceremonies who would interview different children, a famous and comical quick-sketch artist who would invite the children to be artists, a great pantomimist who would act the part of the show's all-around befuddled handyman, plus other wonderful personalities associated with Disney productions.

In addition, worldly-wise to the benefits of cross-promotion, the Disney outline underscored the fact that "The Mickey Mouse Club" TV show would open new horizons in merchandising that would mean new comics, new books, new toys, new record albums, new games, and new kids' apparel.

To look more deeply into how to approach weekly television with the best possible chance for success, Disney commissioned Grant Advertising to prepare an analysis on the proposed "Walt Disney Show." On October 26, 1953, less than a month after the preparation of the Disney preliminary outline, a detailed proposal was submitted by Grant.

"In order to achieve the highest adult and family audience rating for 'The Walt Disney Show,' it must have two basic elements: Subjects are to be selected in accordance with top showmanship values regardless of the category (with the exception of strictly Mickey — saved for his own kid show), and Walt, as our storyteller, providing the key personality contact with the audience and setting the stage for the selected film sequence to follow."

According to the proposal, these key essentials, and all phases of the production, were to be "consistent with the Disney spirit and reputation and not be too elaborate, contrived or juvenile-slanted or lean too heavily upon Walt as a tricky performer. Any attempt to mold his natural friendliness into complicated characterizations or slick emcee professionalism would result in Walt's being infinitely less effective. Walt's storytelling supports should include a basic study and/or workshop set and props that include study furnishings, plus books, maps, globe, models and plans of Disneyland, etc."

The creation of a comprehensive Disney Television Department was another idea offered and outlined in the material "to enable the studio to continually monitor and analyze habits of the viewing audience as well as to be on top of ever-changing trends. Such a department should know all there is to know about the Disney product and its specialized audience appeal, about the studio and its people, about Walt Disney, and about the television industry."

In conclusion, the analysis stated, "The entrance of Walt Disney into television is a revolutionary step — perhaps comparable in importance to his expansion into features. Because of television's incredible impact, it offers an awesome opportunity to charm and entertain millions, and to further the Disney prestige."

Leonard Shannon, a motion picture publicist — or press agent, as they were called at the time — came to work at the Disney Studio in 1954 from RKO just in time to get involved in Disney's new television venture. "The studio was really percolating at that time," he told me. "There was just so much you had to work with. You had animation, you had live action production, you had plans for the Park and you had television. The press was banging down the door to get stories."

Shannon's initial publicity task was "to publicize and make the country aware of Walt in preparation for his debut as a television host," he explained. "Remember, the vast majority of people had never seen him; he was just a guy going through life making movies. But television changed all that."

With the realization that series television would afford him an excellent promotional vehicle for Disney films and his new Park, Walt changed the name of "The Walt Disney Show" to "Disneyland" and structured the format to reflect the Park's themed lands. Thus the show was divided into categories: Adventureland, Fantasyland, Frontierland, and Tomorrowland. There would be cartoons, True-Life Adventure nature films, multi-episode adventures (such as the "Davy Crockett" trilogy), announcements on the progress of Disneyland, and some of the old Disney films.

On October 27, 1954, the TV show "Disneyland" premiered. Walt Disney, in a studylike set, under low-key lighting, greeted the American public. "Good evening, and welcome to the first show of our television series," he said. "Mostly, we're going to tell you stories...tales of adventure and fable drawn from the imagination. And then — we will tell stories of an even more fantastic world...the people and places, the facts of the world we live in today. We hope you like them."

The show, having taken into account all the points made in the Grant Advertising analysis, was an instant hit and a ratings topper for the ABC Television Network. Walt Disney had permanently stepped into our homes and into our lives.

"He became a presence, every week, in your living room," said Shannon. "And Walt enjoyed the recognition. But at the same time,

he lost his anonymity; his ability to listen and talk to people, to get their honest opinions as he could before they knew who he was. But," he added, "the show became a hit and the guy became a star."

About six weeks after the enormously successful premiere of "Disneyland," Walt began moving forward on his ideas for "The Mickey Mouse Club." Based on the outline prepared a year earlier and his own thoughts, Walt scribbled his ideas for the children's show in hastily written abstractions: "Mouse party; audience participation"; "Children selected to be Mickey, Donald, etc. (with costumes), others play the part of Pluto, cat, etc."; "Children from audience visit with characters from history"; "Special shows acted by children in Disneyland"; "Presents to kids in audience with birthdays, also unbirthday presents"; "Drawing lessons"; "Gadget band: kids participate"; "Animal acts"; "Magician"; "Story of children around the world, children in sports (honor Sunday school teachers?)"; "Everyone can sing: song slides."

Robert E. Kintner, then president of the American Broadcasting Company, was in process of conducting discussions with Disney for a "kids' strip" (five-days-a-week programming). A onetime Washington columnist turned broadcasting executive, Kintner was a hard-driving, ferociously competitive man who conducted rounds of dictation with as many as three secretaries at once. He had three television sets in his office, one for each network, and whenever he saw something on his network that displeased him, he promptly fired off a memo to the appropriate party. His record: 35 memos in two days. But as far as Disney was concerned, he was eager to contract with the studio for a quality children's show for ABC television. Following are key excerpts from a confidential memo he sent to Walt Disney on December 16, 1954:

Dear Walt:

I have delayed writing you about the so-called "Disney kids' strip" because I wanted to talk with several advertisers and several agencies about the pricing, character of the show, salability, etc. I received great enthusiasm from the people with whom I talked, and they expressed the belief that the program could be outstanding in television program structure, that it could enable advertisers to expand to the children's group without the criticism of using 'guns and killings' and that with your touch it should be the outstanding daytime programming on all television.

Kintner's letter went on at length describing his ideas for the show, including, among others, time of broadcast, start of season, use of repeats, commercial sale, program format, sponsors, and program appeal. Many of his thoughts were based on the success of kids' strips on radio, which had been the primary broadcast outlet before the onset of television. In that medium, the strength of the kids' strip was that the programs were taped and broadcast at the same time in each of the time zones, 5–6 p.m. local time, a day part that captured the maximum audience of children. Kintner therefore suggested that the Disney show adopt the same pattern for television, a radical approach at the time.

Kintner further explained that ABC-TV would sell advertising time to sponsors in four 15-minute segments on the one-hour show. This would entitle the advertiser to three minutes of commercial in each segment, although he cautioned that "advertisers would be limited to those which appeal directly to children; primarily, cereals, candy, soft drinks, toothpaste and similar products." Disney would then realize $2,500 per quarter-hour segment, with twenty segments Monday through Friday, or $50,000 per week to cover the show's production costs.

"On the content of the program and its format, you would have absolute creative control and deliver to us the package at the agreed upon prices," Kintner stated. "The new program should be designed to appeal to children between the ages of 3 and 14, with the hope that mothers could be picked up as extra audience, but with the basic creative appeal for children.

"I believe that in this 'kids' strip,' there is a potential for the highest rated show in the daytime; for the greatest impact on children in the history of communications; and for the creation of a product that not only will have the enthusiastic support of parents, Parent-Teacher Associations, etc., but will bring a new dimension to daytime programming, one that will satisfy you and be both a creative and a commercial success."

The letter concluded,

> Congratulations on the first Nielsen (for the 'Disneyland' show), which was a 41, with the program reaching 10,832,000 homes. It is 12th on the air in terms of audience. I think this is a terrific job since your rating is higher, according to Nielsen, than the Sid Caesar Show, Godfrey's Talent Scouts and Burns and Allen.
> Sincerely,
> Robert E. Kintner

This memo encouraging Walt to shape the kids' strip was the beginning of what would become a television phenomenon.

The birth and financing of "The Mickey Mouse Club" was tied into the overall expansion of Walt Disney Productions. To assist with this plan, the studio and the ABC Television Network entered into a contract of mutual assistance, which on one side helped Disney progress in the building of Disneyland, thus expanding his corporate holdings, and on the other, helped ABC by providing quality TV programming. "The Mickey Mouse Club," along with Disney's first TV series, "Disneyland," which, as already mentioned, premiered on the ABC Television Network in 1954, provided the basis for that agreement.

The specific financing of "The Mickey Mouse Club," although interrelated with other aspects of this mutual business arrangement, amounted to approximately $14,000,000. The estimated breakdown by year ran: the first year $4,058,000; the second year $5,043,000; the third year $3,102,000 and the fourth year $412,000. ABC made available a million-dollar revolving fund for Walt Disney Productions to turn out "The Mickey Mouse Club" as fast as possible. Filling one hour every day with original material proved demanding and very expensive. But ABC sold the show to many sponsors, which in turn paid the expenses.

Meanwhile, ABC loaned funds to Walt Disney to use for the completion of Disneyland; the figure was reputed to be about $1,500,000. In 1959, Walt Disney settled the broadcasting and Park loans by buying out ABC's interest in the Anaheim, California, Theme Park for $7,500,000.

"The Mickey Mouse Club" series ended new production in 1958, although the show continued in its regular time slot through 1959. But the persistent, sustained interest by the public caused "The Mickey Mouse Club" to be reissued in syndication on a half-hour basis from 1962 through 1965. A critical editing of all previous material for popularity and timeliness, supplemented by new features and serials, shaped the rerelease into a fast-paced, highly marketable children's series for the nationwide station outlets.

In 1962–63, "Mickey Mouse Club" syndication was sold to 119 stations as the first series. In 1963–64, a second series went to 88 stations, and in 1964–65, 57 stations bought the third and final series. The popularity of "The Mickey Mouse Club" adult hosts, Jimmie Dodd and Roy Williams, along with the renown of many of its young stars, including Annette Funicello, Bobby Burgess, Sharon Baird, Cubby O'Brien, and Karen Pendleton, supported the series, and the show again and again proved successful.

Concurrent with this, the foreign television market opened and "The Mickey Mouse Club" was offered internationally. Eighteen countries contracted for the original run of the show, while others bought the syndicated packages. Whenever possible, dubbing of translations in the foreign tongue was used and segments were shown with new audio in Spanish, French, German, Italian, and Japanese.

In Europe, Mickey Mouse marched in Austria (1 year), Belgium (2½ years), Finland (2 years), France (9 years), Italy (7 years), and Switzerland (5 ½ years).

Canada chalked up a total broadcast period of 8 years and 4 months, and in Australia, because of multiple-station use, "The Mickey Mouse Club" overall ran for 14 years. Japan picked it up for almost 3 years, while in Latin America it aired in Chile 3 years, Colombia 1 year, Ecuador 1 year, Mexico 4½ years, and in Panama and Peru, Uruguay, and Venezuela, over 1 year each.

There were many children's shows on television from which to choose to appeal to faithful pint-size viewers. But "The Mickey Mouse Club," with a phenomenal worldwide popularity, still elicits excitement, as is evidenced by a recent comment from a middle-aged fan of the show: "When I was at Disneyland a few years ago for Mickey's sixtieth birthday celebration," she said, "I got to meet several of the original Mouseketeers. I was as excited about that as I was about meeting the Beatles!"

2

A CREATIVE TEAM

I have an organization of people who are really specialists.
You can't match them anywhere in the world
for what they can do. But they all need to be pulled together,
and that's my job.

— WALT DISNEY

BILL WALSH HAD SPENT HALF OF HIS LIFE in show business
before coming to work for Walt Disney Productions. Educated at
the University of Missouri, he had been variously employed as a radio
scriptwriter, reporter, columnist, and press agent. He was fresh from
fifteen years of press agentry with the Ettinger Public Relations
Company when he came to Disney, and it was Walsh whom Disney
selected to mastermind the new show.

Named producer of the "kids' strip" — or "The Mickey Mouse
Club," as it was ultimately named, based on the studio's 1953 early
outline — the former press agent stepped into the role after successfully having produced Disney's first two TV specials as well as the

popular evening series "Disneyland." In the early 1970s, during an interview with a Disney publicist, Walsh explained the rather unusual way he became a producer for Walt.

"Working at the studio, I kept bumping into Walt Disney in the hall or in the parking lot. He used to wonder who is that funny-looking fellow because I was a press agent in those days, and not a very good one. And then one day, in his strange way, he said, 'You, you be the producer of TV.' And I said, 'Huh? I don't have any experience as a producer.' And, with TV still in its infancy, Walt replied, 'Who does?'"

But Disney's instincts were on target, and by the time "The Mickey Mouse Club" came along, Walsh had become a skillful and hardworking producer. Speaking of the time and effort

Bill Walsh, producer of "The Mickey Mouse Club."

that went into the "Disneyland" series, he remarked, "You know, I didn't think we'd get through that first year. Doing a show every week, that was murder." But it was nothing compared to his new task — "an hour show every day. And with children!"

By the end of January 1955, Walsh had prepared a "Mickey Mouse Club" General Format and Preliminary Structure Report, based on Walt's early ideas and Robert E. Kintner's suggestions.

His thoughts included: "By its intent and nature, 'The Mickey Mouse Club' is planned to attract and hold the greatest available children's audience between the ages of three and fourteen, between the hours of 5 and 6 p.m., Monday through Friday.

"Because of our basic ingredients, the names of Walt Disney and Mickey Mouse, the children will expect, and should receive, a substantial measure of cartoon entertainment during the week's shows. I believe we should make reasonably frequent use of these shorts…however, to give the illusion of a lot of cartoon on the show, I believe we should have certain standard sections of animated footage used on all shows as a definite Disney trademark. This regular footage would be used in the opening, the program identification, the Mickey Mouse Club song and the sign-off song.

"Each hour show is divided into four fifteen-minute segments. This appears to be advantageous, both from the multiple sponsors' viewpoint and from our own. The segments should be set up so that they are, in most cases, interchangeable with one another, and can be fitted into other shows on a rerun schedule.

"Scenery, Costumes, Props. In keeping with Disney tradition, I believe our scenery, costumes and props should all be given overall style, good taste, and capable of evoking the utmost in imagination and fun. The sets can be imaginative and fun, without being elaborate.

"Exploitation. As in the parent 'Disneyland' show, proper exploitation of Disney films and merchandise becomes a basic part of our structure.

"Because motion picture film is to play such a large part in 'The Mickey Mouse Club,' it will be necessary to arrange or set up proper production units, here and elsewhere. A preliminary estimate of the amount of film required for our first season's shows may be categorized as follows: Mickey Mouse Newsreels, Mickey Mouse Travelogues, Animal Tales, Safety Films for Children, Sport Reels, 'When I Grow Up' films which will explore possible careers for young folks when they attain adulthood.

"'The Mickey Mouse Club' Cast. The selection of the Mickey Mouse Stock Company — the people who will conduct the Mickey Mouse show onstage from day to day — is of course a vital consideration, and should receive an extended period of screening, auditioning, and a process of trial and error. In our search for Mickey Mouse Club performers, it will be our job to find individuals who best bridge the gap from Disney cartoons to live people in a manner that is believable and entertaining.

"For discussion purposes, a cast structure has been set forth in the following. It is recognized that, as time goes by, our ideas on these cast characters may undergo considerable change. We have given each of them temporary names:

"Smee, the program conductor or general master of ceremonies; Fufu, alternate master of ceremonies; Wilbur, a deadpan artist who never says anything — pantomime is his specialty; Mary Lee, the girl member of the company — she should be pretty, friendly, completely relaxed in the Betty White or Fran Allison tradition; a Genie, 'The Mickey Mouse Club' official magician; Ellsworth, a Talking Mynah Bird; Animal Crackers Orchestra, a group of six musicians and a leader with a large range of flexibility." Eventually, this cast of characters was cut from the show, replaced by the Mouseketeers and two adult hosts.

Walsh also incorporated a mock-up format of Monday-to-Friday programming, with each day falling into a general category — Monday, Travel Night; Tuesday, Participation and Improvement; Wednesday, Musical Night; Thursday, Pets and Hobbies; and Friday, Surprises, Parties, and Contests. These too evolved to the more familiar "Fun with Music Day," "Guest Star Day," "Anything Can Happen Day," "Circus Day," and "Talent Round-Up Day," respectively.

Within a month of Walsh's report, in February, 1955, a joint announcement from ABC's Robert E. Kintner and Roy O. Disney (Walt's brother), president of Walt Disney Productions, confirmed the launch of the new daytime children's series, targeted to begin airing on October 3, 1955.

Putting the pieces together to create the whole and have it on

"Fun with Music Day"

"Talent Round-Up Day"

the air by October 3rd, a mere eight months later, was an extraordinary task facing Walt and Bill Walsh. To begin, they knew that, in addition to the children to be cast on the show, they needed to hire adults who would act as the leaders and authority figures on the program.

"We were looking for talent wherever we could find it," said Walsh. "We were grabbing the janitor right off of his broom. I was going after everything and nothing." But there was a certain redheaded songwriter working in the Disney music department who was about to be thrust into the spotlight. His name was Jimmie Dodd.

A versatile singer-dancer-songwriter, Jimmie was a deeply Christian man who had an irrepressible spirit, a ready smile, and a warm and easygoing personality that would lend itself well to working with children. Born in Cincinnati in

Jimmie Dodd, chosen to host "The Mickey Mouse Club."

1910, he got started in his career when he played banjo with his own combo at the University of Cincinnati. He continued his studies at the Cincinnati Conservatory of Music and rounded out his formal education at the Schouster-Martin School of Dramatic Art in that city.

After moving to St. Petersburg, Florida, Jimmie played guitar and sang his own songs on a radio program on station WSUN. He moved on to Nashville next, and finally settled in California where he toured the nightclub circuit, made appearances with bandleader Louis Prima, and in 1940 broke into motion pictures with the film *Those Were the Days*, starring William Holden.

A heart condition kept Jimmie out of the armed forces during World War II, but he and his wife, former dancer Ruth Carroll, were tireless travelers with the USO. While on an overseas stint, he met television personality Jinx Falkenburg and she was influential in getting him into television in New York, first with Arthur Godfrey and then on her own show. But upon his return to California, his show-business career began to falter and he seriously considered a change.

"He was at the point of getting completely out of show business," explained his wife. "We had come back to California from New York where he had had a very successful year in television. But when we got back to Hollywood it was like every door was closed. We felt that maybe the Lord didn't want him in show business anymore and it was the first time that Jim and I prayed together." Walt Disney was the answer to their prayers.

"The very next day, Bill Justice, one of Disney's director/producers who was an old tennis pal of Jim's, called to say that Walt was looking for a song for his nighttime TV show," Ruth said. "Bill said that Walt loved to animate objects and would like to animate a pencil, but he needed a pencil song. Jim wrote very well on assignment, so he knocked out a song and it was real good." Jimmie made a demo recording of the song, which Bill took to Walt Disney.

"The next thing you know," continued Ruth, "Jim got a call from Jimmy Johnson, the head of the music department, who said, 'We just heard your song. Would you be interested in coming over and talking with us — we might have something to offer you in Music.' So Jim hightailed it over there, and by noon he was signed as a music writer for the studio. They even gave him an office…the first time he ever had one."

While many talented people auditioned for the role of the adult leader of "The Mickey Mouse Club," Bill Walsh and Bill Justice, along with many creative Disney personnel, knew that Jim was the man for the job. But in order for him to win the part, Walsh told him, "We've got to let Walt discover you." And so they plotted to set the boss up.

According to Ruth, "They decided to use the storyboard [a series of rough drawings used to visualize a story, musical number, etc.] for the animated pencil song that Jim had written. They had him come in and perform it for Walt." As if struck by a fantastic notion, after watching the enthusiastic, red-haired songwriter, Walt suddenly proclaimed, "Hey, Jim is the one who should be on 'The Mickey Mouse Club!'" Mission accomplished.

Roy Williams, artist, gagman, and co-adult leader of the club, along with Jimmie Dodd.

In seeking a second-banana adult, again, Walt had just to look in his own backyard to find Roy Williams. With no more than a major in art at Fremont High School, Roy was hired by Disney in 1930 when he was only twenty-three years old. For the first three years of his tenure, Disney paid for his training at the Chouinard Art School in Los Angeles, and then moved him to the studio as an artist on the Mickey Mouse cartoon strips and later into the story department.

"I was a gagman," said Williams. "For a long time all of my work centered around the cartoon shorts. When Walt started working on ideas for the kids' show, he would send ideas to me for gags — you know, to spice them up. He'd come in to show me the script and he'd talk to me about it. Then one day he looked up and said, 'Say, you're fat and funny-lookin', I'm going to put you on "The Mickey Mouse Club" and call you the Big Mooseketeer.'"

Roy was a bit apprehensive. "I was no actor," he said. "And I was scared to death." But he knew if Walt thought it would work, it probably would. "He had a sixth sense," explained Roy. "He knew what people would like. Mostly he knew how to work with creative people to get the utmost of their talent."

To assist in the songwriting for "The Mickey Mouse Club," Walt Disney brought in a young man from Portland, Oregon, named Bob Amsberry. Bob did so well writing tunes for the show that Disney offered him the opportunity to appear on the show. "I didn't think twice about saying 'yes,'" related Amsberry. "I never expected to do anything more than songwriting for Walt and the opportuni-

Bob Amsberry, who appeared on the show in its first years.

ty was like a gift from heaven." Amsberry went on to display a great versatility both in front of the camera and behind the scenes on the first season of "The Mickey Mouse Club."

As activity progressed with the on-air talent, scores of behind-the-scenes production personnel were being hired and assigned the numerous tasks that are required to put together a television show. Among those were writers, directors, choreographers, cameramen, makeup artists, wardrobe people, sound staff, prop and grip departments, set designers, special effects specialists, film editors, and numerous others. In fact, over the course of the four-year run of the show, at least 175 leading directorial, technical, artistic, and administrative personnel staffed "The Mickey Mouse Club."

According to a Walt Disney Company history of "The Mickey Mouse Club," Walt Disney had the final word on policy, criteria of good taste, and all aspects of the continuing productions. He worked with the show constantly. Next to Walt Disney, the overall producer was Bill Walsh. The directors who worked most closely with the Mouseketeers included Dik Darley in the first season, followed for two years by Sidney Miller.

Chuck Keehne, head of the wardrobe department, outfitted the newly hired kids in their Mouseketeer outfits, including their uniquely designed hats, which Roy Williams is credited with creating. "In 1929, after the sound cartoons came out, Walt hired me for two weeks to sketch some ideas for his animated shorts," Roy explained. "One of them had Mickey tipping the top of his head to Minnie, which left him with a flat head. So when 'The Mickey Mouse Club' came about years later, Walt said, 'How do we dress the kids?' And I said, 'Why not with Mickey Mouse ears?' I made sketches of the first hats and Walt liked them. That's how it happened."

"They were beautifully made from soft felt and were wired so the ears wouldn't flop," recalled Annette Funicello. "And you know," she added, "every time we lost a pair we were docked fifty dollars from our paycheck. I personally paid for three pairs, but I guess it was a great way to teach us kids to be responsible."

Overall, the official Mouseketeer costume consisted of soft blue-colored pleated skirts for the girls and matching trousers for the boys, with short-sleeved, ecru-colored turtleneck shirts bearing their names in block black letters across the chest and featuring the circular Mickey Mouse Club logo on the back. Blue matching socks and black tap shoes completed the outfit.

On the evening of September 23, 1955, just ten days before the debut of the show, Walt Disney, in a coast-to-coast 82-station closed-circuit TV preview broadcast from ABC-TV's Studio TV-2 in New York City, described his programming philosophy to the 18 advertisers (and their representatives) who had paid $15,000,000 to sponsor his upcoming series:

"I know, of course, that it's described as a children's show. Yet there's something about the expression 'children's show' that I always find disturbing. At our studio, we regard the child as a highly intelligent human being. He is characteristically sensitive, humorous, open-minded, eager to learn, and has a strong sense of excitement, energy and healthy curiosity about the world in which he lives.

"Lucky indeed is the grownup who manages to carry these same characteristics over into his adult life. It usually makes for a happy and successful individual. Essentially, the real difference between a child and an adult is experience. We conceive it to be our job on 'The Mickey Mouse Club' show to provide some of that experience…happy factual, constructive experience, whenever possible.

"This does not mean to say we are forgetting our chief purpose is entertainment. But we have always tried to be guided by the basic idea that in the discovery of knowledge there is great entertainment —as, conversely, in all good entertainment there is always some grain of wisdom, humanity or enlightenment to be gained."

Segments comprising twenty-two minutes of the upcoming

Monday-through-Friday full-hour series were also previewed for the advertisers, with Walt Disney briefly describing each of them:

"One of these is 'The Mickey Mouse Club Newsreel.' We have our own film-gathering organization, and at the moment, there are between thirty-five and forty camera units in this country and throughout the world shooting material for 'The Mickey Mouse Club Newsreel.' Their job is to report the news — to give our children a factual viewpoint on the things that are going on in the world about them — the things that interest and concern them now, and the things that will have a bearing in the future.

"Our old friend Jiminy Cricket will also be part of the show. Jiminy's going to help us with what we call our factual entertainment. He'll show the youngsters things about the living world, about health, hygiene, safety and many other things that concern their well-being.

"Every day, Monday through Friday, in the second quarter-hour segment of the show, we are starring our own 'Mickey Mouse Club' Mouseketeers...likeable youngsters of whom we are very proud. We believe many of the great show-business entertainers of tomorrow will come from this and succeeding companies of Mouseketeers. Their job is, of course, to sing, dance and generally regale the home audience with entertainment. They will have guest stars, personalities, circus and novelty acts. But they will make it their special business to introduce youthful talent from every part of the world. Again, we feel, there is a strong secondary value here — in that watching the Mouseketeers and their guests in action, boys and girls in homes throughout the land will feel impelled to discover and develop their own talents, whatever they may be.

"The third quarter-hour segment of the show gives us a chance to try a number of storytelling ideas. First, we plan to bring back that story technique we all knew and loved as kids — the continued story, or as it was known then, the serial. Secondly, in this segment we will tell stories of children in other nations — England, France, Italy, Ireland, Japan, Samoa, Scandinavia, and others. Third, we'll go on exploring expeditions. Here, too, in this third segment will be our 'What I Want to Be' series, in which youngsters can explore the profession in which they are most interested. It will give them firsthand knowledge of the facts and fascination in the work where their future and success may lie. Finally," Disney concluded, "the Mouseketeers will return to present our cartoon of the day."

Robert E. Kintner summed up the presentation, saying, "You are buying more than a great franchise on a most important show. You will be able to capitalize on the greatest reservoir of good will in America — Walt Disney."

3
TALENT ROUND-UP

Saddle your pony, here we go…
— Lyrics "Mickey Mouse Club"
Talent Round-Up song

TO SEARCH FOR THE CHILDREN WHO WOULD STAR on "The Mickey Mouse Club," Walt Disney was quietly scouting Hollywood and environs. Bill Walsh had suggested to Walt that they just start calling up some of the professional schools to find the kids. But Walt had different ideas. "Wait a minute, hold it," he told Walsh. "I don't want to go to any of those professional schools. I don't want those kids that tap-dance or blow trumpets while they're tap-dancing or skip rope or have curly hair like Shirley Temple or nutty mothers. I just want ordinary kids."

Walsh protested, "But, Walt, what if they can't do anything?" "Then we'll teach them," Walt said. "Go to a school and watch the kids at recess. Watch what happens to you. You'll notice that you're watching one kid. Not any of the other kids, but sooner or later your gaze will always go back to this one kid. That kid has star quality. Not a lot of star quality, maybe, but there's always a reason why you're watching that one kid. That's the kid we want to get in 'The Mickey Mouse Club.'"

According to an internal memo from Walt Disney, dated April 15, 1955, the talented kids of "The Mickey Mouse Club" were to be called Mouseketeers. However, it was not the first use of the word. Apparently, Disney had coined the expression for a 1936 Silly Symphony cartoon, "Three Blind Mouseketeers," and had allowed MGM to use it in a cartoon short, starring well-known animation stars Tom and Jerry, entitled "The Two Mouseketeers." Since that time, Western Printing had produced, and Dell had distributed, three one-shot comic magazines using the word. In August of 1955, the Disney Studio was made aware that MGM had completed two additional cartoon shorts for which they were once again going to use the term "Mouseketeer."

Through mutual agreement with MGM, the Hollywood studio consented not to use the word in any future short subjects. Both Western Publishing and Dell also agreed to the same as far as any future publications were concerned. In the meantime, however, for legal protection Disney trademarked the word "Mouseketeer."

The audition process began in March 1955, as hundreds of children streamed through the gates at Walt Disney Productions. They came from schoolyards, and, contrary to Walt's original inclinations, from local talent contests, amateur shows, and neighborhood dancing schools. A few had worked professionally, but by and large they came from non-showbusiness families and were, therefore, largely unspoiled and innocent of any pampering or egocentric behavior.

Lee Traver and Jack Lavin, the casting directors, brought the kids in while Jimmie Dodd, Roy Williams, and Bill Walsh worked together at making the selections. Walt Disney gave most of the applicants a careful personal screening for personality, poise, appearance, and musical ability.

Jimmie Dodd chats with the many children waiting to audition.

"The first person you saw when you went to audition was Jack Lavin," explained Bobby Burgess, an original Mouseketeer who is best remembered by his big, broad smile and daily appearance on every "Mickey Mouse Club" show from beginning to end. "He was a heavyset guy who always bit his tongue. I remember he wore big old suspenders and he'd always lean back in his chair and talk to you. Lee

A young boy, one of many hundreds, auditions for "The Mickey Mouse Club."

Traver was interesting, too," he remarked to me. "He was a gray-haired man and more serious and hands-on when it came to auditioning."

A typical audition sheet listed the child's name, age, where recruited from, and their talents. For example, Bobby was listed as "age 13, Dances, Tap, Ballet, submitted by agent Hazel MacMillan." There were eleven others listed on his particular audition sheet, including Darlene Gillespie and Doreen Tracey, both also destined to join the Mouseketeer ranks. One unfortunate youngster, a 9-year-old named Gregory Littler, apparently didn't make his audition. A simple handwritten notation next to his name read "chicken pox."

Bobby came to his audition having appeared in seventy-five amateur shows. "I started dancing when I was about four," he said. "And I had my first dancing partner at five. Then I did amateur shows and won all kinds of prizes like aquariums, watches, and bicycles." Bobby's initial call to the Disney Studio was not Mouseketeer-connected. "Originally, I went out for 'Spin and Marty' [which became a popular serial on the show], but didn't make it," he said. "Then they asked me if I could sing and dance. Of course I said yes." Finally, Bobby auditioned five times, and won over the selection panel by dancing barefoot to a jazz version of "Rock Around the Clock."

Darlene Gillespie, one of the most popular members of the "core" group (those who appeared on the program for the entire four-year run) recounted her audition twenty years later on an NBC nighttime talk show. "I went down there, very honestly, by accident with a group of other girls who had been called in, because I wanted to see what the Disney Studio looked like," she said. "And I did a little dance number because I had taken dancing lessons with these four other girls, and then they said to us, because I guess they were looking for rounded talents, 'Can any of you sing?'

"I was really very innocent about it and said, 'Sure.'" Fourteen-year-old Darlene sang "The Ballad of Davy Crockett." "I liked that song," she said, "and I guess they did too, because the next thing you know, they chose me to be a Mouseketeer."

Roy Williams recalled the audition process. "Jimmie Dodd, Bill Walsh, and I picked them out. I had a big easel there and I would roughly sketch the different kids doing their act with their names underneath, so we would remember if they were doing ballet or singing or dancing," Roy said. "The sketches didn't look like them, they were sort of shorthand drawings. Plus we took photographs of the kids."

Carl "Cubby" O'Brien was one of the youngest kids chosen to be on the show. "I was eight when I first auditioned," he said. "I remember showing up along with hundreds of kids." Cubby, a talented drummer who was following in his dad's footsteps, was discovered at a charity show. "My father was a drummer," he said. "And one Christmas we were invited to the Screen Actors Guild Children's Christmas Fund. I was sick and had a one-hundred-and-three-degree temperature and wasn't going to go. But at the last minute I felt a little better, went to the show, and played a drum solo wearing a straw hat. Several producers from Disney were at the event and I was called in to audition."

Although Cubby was talented, he had no performing experience other than drumming. "I had never sung or danced in my life," he said. "At the audition I played drums but I remember Jimmie saying, 'Would you sing something for us?' 'I'm not a singer,' I said. 'Well, sing "Happy Birthday."'" A banjo player on the stage played the intro, "dah, dah, dah, dah, dah, dah," as Cubby launched into the simple song every kid knew, but for this kid, being able to carry the tune won him a spot on the Mouseketeer roster.

Cubby was immediately paired with another of the youngest audition winners: corkscrew-curled, blonde, blue-eyed Karen Pendleton. "Like a lot of the others, it was through my dancing school that I auditioned for the show," Karen said. "I was eight and didn't have a clue what was going on. I just did my little dance, except I do remember that I got the giggles right in the middle of it. Then I looked over at some of the people in the room and I recognized Jimmie Dodd. He had sung at my church just the previous Sunday." As Karen recalls, she was hired with one audition.

Two of the more professional children selected to appear on the show were Sharon Baird and Lonnie Burr. Sharon started dancing at the age of three, and just a few years later her legs were insured for $50,000. She explained: "Eddie Cantor was looking for young dancers

Roy Williams and Jimmie Dodd review some of the Mouseketeer finalists.

for his 'Colgate Comedy Hour' television show. So I auditioned and although I was too short for what they had in mind, they wrote a special part for me, signed me to a contract, and insured my legs for fifty thousand dollars!"

Sharon, who was born in Seattle, had launched her career in the Little Miss America Pageant by winning for the state of Washington and competing in California in the nationals. "I came in second," she said, "but my mom loved the area so much, she persuaded my dad to move down." The move proved beneficial. "After 'The Colgate Comedy Hour,' I did a lot of television shows like 'Death Valley Days' and 'The Donald O'Connor Show.' Those led to a film called *Artists and Models*, with Dean Martin and Jerry Lewis."

It was Sharon's involvement in the Martin and Lewis film that led to her audition for "The Mickey Mouse Club." "I was at Capitol Records for a recording session on the film," she said, "and was seen by Jimmie Dodd, who recommended me to Disney." Twelve-year-old Sharon's dancing, especially her tap-dancing ability, plus her warm demeanor and personality, secured her spot on the show.

Young show-business veteran Lonnie Burr was slick, professional, and keenly precocious. Born in Dayton, Kentucky, to vaudeville dancing team "Dot and Dash," Lonnie relocated with his parents to Los Angeles when he was three and started working professionally as a singer, dancer, and actor at age five. "I did films and then went on to TV to do a variety of shows, including a recurring role on 'The Ruggles' show,' " Lonnie said. "I also did commercials and performed in live shows." Lonnie was twelve when he auditioned and was hired to join the children's troupe on "The Mickey Mouse Club."

Tryouts for the new television program brought in its share of pint-sized musicians and dancers. Good kid singers, however, were hard to come by. For 13-year-old Tommy Cole, crooning assured him a spot on the program. "My music teacher got me the audition," Tommy explained. "I played the accordion with about five or six other accordionists, and I sang. I was the only singer, and Lee Traver, the casting director, picked me out. Within three months, I went through two or three auditions and was then signed to a trial contract. It was 'trial' at first because even though they liked my voice, they wanted to see if I could learn to dance. So what they did was give me concentrated dancing lessons every day. I guess it worked."

"I had just turned eleven when I first auditioned to be a Mouseketeer," recalled Doreen Tracey. "My dad had a dancing studio

Tommy Cole, "The Mickey Mouse Club" crooner.

called the Rainbow Studio. And one day I happened to be sitting behind the desk watching the phones when a call came in from Jack Lavin, the casting director at Disney Studio. He asked about getting some of the kids from the school out to audition for a new Disney show." Following the example of her parents, a top show-business

37

THE ORIGINAL MOUSEKETEERS

SHARON

Sharon Baird

BOBBY

Bobby Burgess

LONNIE

Lonnie Burr

Tommy Cole

Annette Funicello

Darlene Gillespie

Cubby O'Brien

Karen Pendleton

Doreen Tracey

dance team during the '30s and '40s called "Tracey and Hay," Doreen loved performing and had been doing so since she was a young child. Hearing about this audition was like a dream come true. "Oh, I know a little girl who would be just perfect for your auditions," she told Lavin. After talking with her father, Doreen was on her way to the audition.

"It was held in the studio commissary," she said. "It was a cattle call, jammed full of kids. I remember it was rainy and sticky that day and the room smelled of little people." Accompanied by her own piano player with her own music, Doreen performed a song called "Cross Over the Bridge," a popular hit tune by singer Patti Page about an ill-fated love affair. "I thought it would be funny for a little girl to be singing about such a grown-up thing," she said. "I had a big hoop skirt and whenever I hit certain words I'd flip the little skirt to each side to show my pantaloons. For the big finish, I did a split." Confident in her performance, she said, "I knew I had the job." Before long, she was notified that she had indeed been hired.

The other first-year Mouseketeers selected were: Nancy Abbate, Billie Jean Beanblossom, Dennis Day, Mary Espinosa, Bonni Lou Kern, Mary Lynn Sartori, Bronson Scott, Michael Smith, Mark Sutherland, Don Underhill, Johnny Crawford, Dickie Dodd, Judy Harriet, John Lee Johann, and Ronnie Steiner. There were also three young men who would never make it beyond the first days of filming. Paul Petersen, later to gain fame as Jeff Stone on "The Donna Reed Show," was dismissed for disruptive behavior. "I became the first ex-Mouseketeer," admitted Petersen, "fired for conduct unbecoming." Mickey Rooney Jr. and Tim Rooney, sons of the well-known actor, were released after a particularly mischievous and unruly foray into the Disney paint department.

The roster of children thus far cited became the first twenty-three chosen. The twenty-fourth and final Mouseketeer to be signed to the show was a young lady discovered by Walt Disney himself. Her name was Annette Funicello.

"I was twelve years old and dancing the lead in *Swan Lake* at the Starlight Bowl in Burbank," Annette said. "Unannounced, Walt Disney was in the audience that night." Virginia Funicello, Annette's mother, added, "The very next day her dancing school got a call from Lee Traver, a Disney casting director. He said they'd like to see the little black-haired girl who played the Swan Queen, to audition for 'The Mickey Mouse Club.'" The Funicellos were so totally removed from show business that Virginia remarked, "I didn't even know what an audition was!"

In addition, because her daughter was so painfully shy, Virginia said to Al Gilbert, Annette's dancing teacher, who called with the news, "Oh no, my daughter will never go in a million years." When she asked Annette about it, the child's response was not unexpected. "No, no, no, I don't want to go!"

"I was so shy as a child, my parents tell me that every time the doorbell rang, I used to run and hide, either under my bed or in the closet," Annette explained. "In fact, that's the reason I took dancing lessons, to help overcome my shyness." Because Annette was so fond of her teacher, he managed to convince her to go to the audition "just for the experience of it."

"We'd never been in a studio in our life," Virginia said. "I was scared to death." She recalled sitting quietly in the back of the room while a menagerie of kids took their turn performing. "I was next to this group of men and I didn't know who any of them were. One of them turned to me as Annette was auditioning and said, 'Who is that little girl with the black hair? She's dynamite.' I said, 'That's my daughter' — real scared, you know, I thought they didn't like her."

On the way home in the car, Al Gilbert told Annette, "There were so many children there, I don't know if you stand a chance or not, but you did a good job and I'm proud of you." He needn't have questioned the impression she had made on the Disney people. The very next day, Annette's dancing school once again heard from Disney casting. "They wanted to hire her for two weeks to test her out," said Virginia. "If they liked her, they would put her under contract. Well, she was there for the two weeks and they loved her. In fact, she stayed under contract for ten years."

4
LEARNING THE ROPES

He [Walt Disney] refuses to limit his field of operations.
He has a firm faith in his own infallibility.
He has a patience that is quite indifferent
to the sure bet and the quick return.

— NEWSWEEK

IN 1955, LIFE AT THE WALT DISNEY STUDIO was very much akin to working on a college campus. Even today, with the bustle of activity that exists in the company that has become a diverse entertainment giant, the look and feel of the place is the same, manicured and tranquil. The studio's main thoroughfare is named Mickey Avenue with the center cross-street Dopey Drive, as it was over five decades ago. Except for the addition of two new office structures and the transformation of the back-lot sets to a trailer park of mini-offices, on the surface nothing has changed.

For the newly installed Mouseketeers, the well-tended studio pathways, with their freshly planted flowers and ample wide-open grassy spaces, provided the ideal workplace for a young performer. Their primary "home," however, was to be Soundstage One, the set of "The Mickey Mouse Club." Stationed directly outside the warehouse-like structure were their "little red schoolhouses," two trailers painted cherry red, in which they were to be educated daily while working on the show.

But before they could set foot on the lot as talent, there were many legalities to be taken care of. First was signing the contract (also signed by a parent or guardian), which served as the Agreement between Walt Disney Productions and the "Artist." The document, all twelve single-spaced pages of it, explained in finite legal detail precisely the terms and conditions of employment.

The intersection of Mickey Avenue and Dopey Drive on the Disney Studio lot.

SIGNING ON THE DOTTED LINE

The following is the opening paragraph of the Mouseketeers' contract (in this case, Mouseketeer Sharon Baird):

"AGREEMENT made as of the 16th day of May, 1955 between WALT DISNEY PRODUCTIONS, A California Corporation, hereinafter called 'Producer,' and SHARON BAIRD, hereinafter called 'Artist':

1. (a) The Producer hereby employs Artist to act, play, sing, dance, perform, rehearse and take part in the production of motion picture photoplays with or without synchronized words, dialogue, songs and music and whether for exhibition in theatres or on television; in performances on the stage before an audience, in vaudeville and in personal appearances in theatres and other places of entertainment, in radio broadcastings, in live television, and in performances for transmission on television; in recording the Artist's voice and performance for reproduction and/or transmission by any means or methods now known or which may hereafter be devised; and in connection with any and all the foregoing to render speaking parts and/or musical numbers and/or such other routine and business, and such other services, consistent with the Artist's talents and abilities, as the Producer may assign to the Artist. All of said services shall be performed by the Artist for and as directed by the Producer at its studios in Burbank, California and/or at such other studios and such other places and/or on such locations as the Producer may from time to time designate."

The sixty-nine paragraphs that followed, along with the required signatures and approval by the Los Angeles Superior Court, sealed the deal that was to pay each Mouseketeer the sum of $185 per 48-hour six-day (Monday–Saturday) week. By stipulation of the Court, Walt Disney Productions was directed to withhold 15% of the gross compensation payable to the minors to be devoted to the purchase of United States Savings Bonds in their names, with their mothers named as beneficiary. The bonds were held in trust until each child's twenty-first birthday.

The producer had the option, at 26-week intervals, to renew the contract with an increase in salary which, after ten options, could reach a weekly rate of $500. Although by today's standards it may seem that the Mouseketeers were being paid less than one might expect, it was 1955, and in many cases their income exceeded that of their parents.

With regard to the Monday–Friday part of their work week, the Los Angeles Board of Education had very specific rules and regulations that governed the studio in relation to children and schoolwork. It specified that minors aged six and over employed in the motion picture industry were permitted eight hours a day on the lot (four hours' work, three hours' school, and one hour lunch/recreation). Regulations also stated that the children would not be permitted to remain on the lot after 6 p.m., and schooling was to be completed not later than 4 p.m. The Board of Education, however, gave some leeway to the producer during the summer months and on non-school days, permitting the use of children on the basis of six hours of work within an eight-hour day.

Additionally, in all instances, a teacher/welfare worker, supplied by the Los Angeles Board of Education, had to be employed when children were called in for production. On school days, one such individual was required for each ten children. On weekends and school

The little red schoolhouse trailers.

holidays, one was required for each group of twenty children. At the time, teacher/welfare workers were paid on the basis of $29 per day, or $144.38 if employed by the week.

Then there was the matter of securing a work permit. "In order to get a work permit, we had to go down to the Board of Education," said Bobby Burgess. "We had to show them that we weren't nervous and biting our fingernails or anything like that." Annette's mom, Virginia, remembered, "If they thought there were any problems caused by work stress, the kids would lose their permit. And they had to go down there every six months to have it renewed."

At the studio, organizing the twenty-four Mouseketeers posed special problems, particularly related to school time versus work time. To accomplish the task of producing five one-hour shows per week, production had to move with lightning speed or else deadlines could not be met. Therefore, in an effort to maximize availability of all Mouseketeers, they were divided into three groups, the red, the white, and the blue. The first team, red (ultimately the key group of Mouseketeers seen in the show openings and closings every day), worked mornings while the second team, white, attended school in the trailers and the third team, blue, rehearsed. Thus, with organized scheduling of show segments, the production team was able to utilize Mouseketeers throughout the entire workday.

"It was hysteria," said Bill Walsh. "It was like a Chinese fire drill. But it was fun because we'd have meetings in the morning with the kids, then we'd meet with the writers, then with the guys who did the sets and the costumes. After lunch everyone would meet again. By that time, we all would contribute ideas about props, sets, wardrobe, music, and about three o'clock that afternoon we'd shoot it. It was fresh; you didn't have time to get over-rehearsed."

Meanwhile, the signed sponsors were eagerly awaiting the promised financial rewards to be reaped from Walt Disney's entry into children's television. Ninety-eight TV stations across the country, representing 93.8% of all U.S. TV homes, had been lined up to broadcast the new series, which would showcase their commercial messages to America's youngsters.

In a survey completed April 1954, Advertest, Inc. (a research firm), found that children had become major influences as to what went into the family market basket.

The study reported that out of 561 parents interviewed, 73.1% said that they had been asked to buy at least one product that was advertised on a children's program. Of these parents, 93.9% made the purchase.

Television magazine noted in an October 1954 article, titled "Don't Sell the Kids' Shows Short," that "case history after case history is available to document the fact that children are by far the most receptive group to television advertising, and this goes beyond 5-cent candy bars. It encompasses products whose use will increase as young viewers become adults."

Among the first products to be presented included: Ipana toothpaste from Bristol Myers (who can forget Bucky Beaver [voiced by Jimmie Dodd] singing, "Brusha, brusha, brusha. Brusha with Ipana!"); Armour & Company hot dogs, sausages, and dog food; Campbell soups; Mars candy bars; Coca-Cola; TV Time popcorn; Welch's jams, jellies, and grape juice; and General Mills' variety of cake mixes and cereals, including Wheaties, Cheerios, Trix, Kix, and Sugar Jets. In addition, Walt Disney Productions was available to advertisers to produce their commercials for "The Mickey Mouse Club," subject to negotiation and at additional fees. Several of the advertisers, including General Mills, Carnation, and Mattel, did so.

The Mouseketeers, uninvolved in the business aspects of the show, were becoming acquainted with their new environment. "It was a funny feeling to be at the studio during the first days of shooting 'The Mickey Mouse Club,'" Bobby Burgess remarked. "Here we were little kids that came onto this huge soundstage and it made me feel real small. And we just started dancing and singing and kind of figuring out what they wanted us to do.

"We had to learn so many things — like lighting, for example. They had what was called the 'central arc.' I remember it was so important to learn how to get in that central arc. And the director would say, 'Okay, hit the arc,' and this big, huge thing would light up."

"I remember the first day we were shooting and the director calling, 'Cut!'" said Karen Pendleton. "And I thought to myself, What is he doing, we're right in the middle of a television show and he's stopping! I didn't know it was being shot on film and we were supposed to stop and start."

The Mouseketeers' overall time at the studio was guided by a "call sheet." The children's names were listed along the left-hand side of the sheet and next to it the time they had to be in, the time to report to the set, end-of-the-day dismissal time, and hours out for meals. At the end of each day, they would receive their call sheet for the following day.

Production had begun in May 1955 and by the end of July an astounding 56 eleven-minute-five-second Mouseketeer segments had been shot. As Hal Adelquist, a production coordinator on the show, stated in a memo to Walt Disney, "This constitutes production effort in the first 10 weeks of shooting." Included were production numbers and openings for "Fun with Music Day," "Guest Star Day," "Anything Can Happen Day," "Circus Day," and "Talent Round-Up Day."

Finally, after eight months of intense and harried preparation, "The Mickey Mouse Club" made its debut on Monday, October 3, 1955. Broadcast from 5 p.m. to 6 p.m. in all time zones across the country, the show opened, with its first segment "The Mickey Mouse Club Newsreel." Featured that first day were stories that were headlined "Boys Brave Buzz Boats" — a thrilling boat ride into the Florida Everglades; "The Music Goes 'Round" — a children's orchestra in Italy playing Disney's "Bibbidi Bobbidi Boo"; and a World Report Mouseketeer News section highlighted by news film covering stories in England, Italy, Tokyo, and Burbank, California (featuring a Disney

Studio visit, with Fess Parker and Buddy Ebsen filming the "Davy Crockett" series).

The second segment starred the Mouseketeers in "Fun with Music Day," dancing and singing to two numbers, "Friendly Farmers" and "The Shoe Song." The third segment presented a TWA film serial entitled "What I Want to Be," illustrating what it was like to be a pilot and to be an airline hostess. The fourth segment brought on several Mouseketeers to introduce, in song, the Cartoon of the Day: "Time to twist our Mousekedial, to the right and the left with a great big smile. This is the way we get to see, the Mousecartoon for you and me!" The mouse-eared kids then turned about-face to the Mickey Mouse Treasure Mine set and recited, "Meeska, mooska, Mouseketeer; Mousecartoon time now is here!" From the Disney treasure chest of shorts came "Pueblo Pluto."

Following was the show's everyday finale. The nine red-team Mouseketeers, seated under a Mickey Mouse banner, with Jimmie Dodd and Roy Williams standing beside them, slowly and reverently sang the song baby boomers and generations to follow will never forget: "Now it's time to say goodbye to all our company. M-I-C ["See ya real soon," recited Jimmie Dodd], K-E-Y ["Why, because we *like* you," he declared], M-O-U-S-E!"

Just before the show credits and music rolled, an animated Mickey said the final goodbyes, reminding us to tune in the following day. "Thanks, Mouseketeers, for joining the party. Now tomorrow, 'Guest Star Day,' it's our big show! Bye all!"

On Tuesday morning, October 4, the initial rating results were in. According to the first Trendex 15-city report, the program was doing better than NBC and CBS combined. Based on its first ratings, "The Mickey Mouse Club" had made a meteoric debut and its effect on the competition was devastating. In its premiere week, the show had an advantage of 93% over NBC's "Pinky Lee Show," and an 83% edge over NBC's "Howdy Doody Show," according to the Nielsen

Ratings Service national data. An ABC-TV press release boasted that "ABC-TV's 'Mickey Mouse Club' is the highest rated regular daytime television program."

What specifically did the viewing audience like about the show? For purposes of investigating viewing of "The Mickey Mouse Club," during the week of October 14–23, 749 New York metropolitan area television homes were interviewed by Advertest. Questioning was conducted with adults who viewed the program, regardless of whether children viewed, and with children between five and sixteen years old who regularly viewed and were at home.

The results of the analysis showed that the cartoons were an overwhelming favorite among both adults and children. Only teenagers did not rank the cartoons as their favorite. The "Nature of Things" (a filmed series on animal life-styles) was their choice. One of the major items mentioned by adults in listing their reasons for liking "The Mickey Mouse Club" was that it was educational.

Comparing six top children's programs in the New York metropolitan area — "Pinky Lee," "Howdy Doody," "Barker Bill," "Merry Mailman," "Big Top," and "Super Circus" — the respondents were asked whether they liked "The Mickey Mouse Club" more, less, or the same as each of the other programs. In every case, "The Mickey Mouse Club" was liked more, among all age groups questioned.

"The Mickey Mouse Club Newsreel" was the second highest ranking favorite of the total group of respondents, following on the heels of the cartoon feature. Interesting, at this early stage the Mouseketeers ranked extremely low on the "best liked" scale among both adults and children participating in the survey.

Walt never underestimated the opinions of the viewing audience and a detailed breakdown report on "Mickey Mouse Club" fan mail was submitted to him each week (with copies for an additional thirty to forty "Mickey Mouse Club" personnel). Each report contained information that specifically listed the number of letters received, separated by individual request; i.e., how many letters requested photos, how many commented on the show or had criticisms, what miscellaneous questions were asked, etc. The report also listed interesting excerpts from letters.

In the first few weeks of the show, contrary to the Advertest survey, the Mouseketeers' popularity began to grow, as did the renown of the show itself, adding millions of viewers to its successful debut. Early fan mail largely consisted of kids writing in requesting membership cards for "The Mickey Mouse Club," asking for photos, wanting more information about the Mouseketeers, and some unusual requests as well.

Excerpts from the first month's mail included:

Dear Mickey: Could I be one of your Mouseketeers? Tell me how I can be one. I would like to join the fun.

Today I saw your program and I saw the dance some children did. It was a western dance. The children were riding play ponies. Halloween will soon be here. My mother is going to make a cowgirl suit for me so I wondered if you could send me one of those ponies. I would be very happy if you could.

How did those kids get to be a Mouseketeer? I'd love to be one. I never missed their show once. I'd like to be a Mouseketeer more than have a bike.

I am 12 years old and I have a trained rooster who can do lots of tricks: 1) open a birthday present; 2) be hypnotized; 3) walk a fence; 4) talk (in chicken chatter); 5) balance on top of my head upside down. He can do many more things. I've had him since he was a little chicken.

I can sing and have been taking dancing lessons for five years. Is it possible for me to become a member of "The Mickey Mouse

Club"? Do my parents have to be actors or actresses? Do I have to be wealthy?

Dear Jimmy: I would like to have a picture of one of the Mouseketeers. I want to have a picture of Annette.

A girlfriend of mine and I would like to know if on Round-Up day in about four weeks we could be on your show. We would like to sing. Our ages are 10 and 11 and we live in Lansing, Michigan.

I watch your show, "The Mickey Mouse Club," but there's one thing I don't like about it and that is that it's too short. It seems the minute I turn it on, it's over. That is because I like it so much.

Thank you so much for my freedom between 5 and 6 p.m. every day! For that one heavenly hour I'm sure my kiddies will be glued to one safe spot — directly before the TV screen and your delightful "Mickey Mouse Club" program. My small-fry are the usual normal variety of kiddies (meaning they carry on like so many squirrels) so it is a real compliment to your TV show that it offers enough variety to enchant them into sitting still!

By the end of October, when the show had been on the air for a month, fan mail was steadily on the increase, with more and more of it arriving at the Disney Studio each day. As the mail multiplied, so did the popularity of the Mouseketeers. To pre-teeners across the nation, the mouse-eared youngsters were about to become adolescent superstars.

REVIEWS

"There's never been anything like MICKEY MOUSE to hit television.... There's enough here to keep the kiddies in every household glued to their sets most every afternoon.... Jimmie Dodd and the kids are certainly finds — finds in the sense of talent — every one of them can sing, dance and in tandem they're great.... About the best of four segments on the preem show...was the 'What I Want to Be' serialized stanza, with the career kickoffer dealing with airline pilots and hostesses.... Stirling Silliphant, who's one of the overall production supervisors on the show, scripts this segment and does a fine and gentle job of it.... MICKEY MOUSE CLUB should have no trouble at all knocking the pants off the competition in the 5-6 period. It's the kiddies who rule the television tuners at that hour, and it's a good bet they'll insist on ABC, which should make Disney, ABC and a host of sponsors quite happy."

— *Variety*

"The show yesterday had a rousing opener with cartoon characters playing a lively march. There's a lot of good children's music coming up on the show.... The children's newsreel was good stuff, with a lot of interesting information.... The closer was surefire, and will continue to be, an old Disney cartoon."

— New York *Post*

"MICKEY MOUSE CLUB unveiled its junior jukebox of pint-size delights with some suitably charming Walt Disney daffiness and ingenious diversion.... It was several cuts above the customary noisy nonsense deployed by Pinky Lee and Howdy Doody for about the same audiences."

— King Features

"ABC-TV's Mickey Mouse Club is a smash box office hit, no doubt about that."

— New York *Daily News*

"The filling of five hours a week of entertainment is a massive enterprise which only the Disney empire could contemplate with equanimity. It's been tackled with great ingenuity...the show is studded with tidbits designed to enrich little minds or improve little characters....The cartoons from Mr. Disney's vast treasure trove are enchanting. And many of the other features are good clean fun."

— JOHN CROSBY, syndicated columnist

"Moreover, it's the type of show that will appeal to adults, not those with a juvenile mind, but those who enjoy children — enjoy watching them at play, at work and growing up....His [Disney's] knack of touching exactly the right spot all the time is nigh phenomenal."

— *Billboard*

"Consensus of opinion is that the network will be forced to set up some sort of repeat schedule in the evening hours so that grown-ups may be able to see the show, too. It has great adult as well as child appeal."

— New York *World-Telegram & Sun*

There was one important review, however, that was not so kind. In fact, it was downright scathing. The piece was written by Jack Gould and it appeared in *The New York Times* on Tuesday, October 4. The following is his complete critique:

Walt Disney's long-awaited afternoon show for children, 'The Mickey Mouse Club,' had its premiere yesterday on Channel 7. Hopeful parents, who had assumed that Mr. Disney would bring about a long-needed revolution in adolescent TV programming, can only keep their fingers crossed. His debut bordered on the disastrous.

Not only was the opening show roughly on a par with any number of existing displays of juvenile precocity, but Mr. Disney and the American Broadcasting Company went commercial to a degree almost without precedent. In the sixty minutes between 5 and 6 o'clock there were twenty commercials, one of which burst smack in the middle of a 'Pluto' cartoon. This viewer cannot recall ever having seen a children's program — or an adult's for that matter — that was quite as commercial as Mr. Disney's, which is easily the new season's most distressing news. Apparently even a contemporary genius is not immune to the virus of video.

Just as the result of an opening game does not determine the ultimate winner of a world series, so too, in television a premiere is not always a clue to the quality of a continuing series. Perhaps Mr. Disney will quickly put matters in order. But, unlike the opening of his evening show, 'Disneyland,' which was such a happy augury of things to come, the premiere of 'The Mickey Mouse Club' was both keenly disheartening and disappointing.

To look on the bright side of things first, Mr. Disney obviously has potentially a great feature in his 'children's newsreel.' The British Broadcasting Corporation has had a magnificent such newsreel for many years, and apparently 'The Mickey Mouse Club' will now offer the American equivalent. It is high time. Yesterday's glimpse of a visit to a Seminole village in Florida and a young orchestral group in Rome were fine.

Though the introductory installment was produced with all the know-how of the nickelodeon era, Mr. Disney should be able to pull out of the fire his feature on different occupations, beginning with the jobs of an airline pilot and an airline hostess.

But much of the premiere — and apparently much of the future programs to be seen on Mondays through Fridays — will be devoted to a group known as the Mouseketeers, led by Jimmie Dodd. This group of youngsters evidently was borrowed from the children's amateur hours around the country. Their production numbers yesterday were only irritatingly cute and contrived and bereft of any semblance of the justly famous Disney touch.

There was also an episode involving the 'Friendly Farmer,' which turned out to be a prolonged and dreary marathon of barnyard noises. This sort of familiar nonsense will not woo the tots away from 'Howdy Doody' nor the young adult from the afternoon western and mystery movies.

In fact, Mr. Disney's opening show clearly suggests that he is trying to appeal to children of all ages between 6 and 16, which has been the graveyard of more than one show intended for the younger generation.

One of Hollywood's most imaginative minds should not be led astray by the makers of soft drinks and breakfast cereals who were the stars of his premiere. Both young viewers and their parents are anticipating the very best that Mr. Disney can provide and nothing less.

Let us hope that this will be forthcoming. Mickey Mouse's fans certainly will be patient and will reserve judgment for some weeks to come. But yesterday, Mr. Disney momentarily let everyone down, very far down."

On that same day, Walt Disney received a wire from New York:

Dear Walt:

I saw "The Mickey Mouse Club" and enjoyed it, and if my friends and acquaintances, including my six-year-old and twelve-year-old are an indication, the show should go very well.

While it does not bother me as far as ratings are concerned, Jack Gould of *The New York Times* blasted the show including the Mouseketeers. I am sure he will be proved wrong.

— Robert E. Kintner

One month later, the Nielsen November 1 report ratings showed "The Mickey Mouse Club" to be the new king of daytime TV, "holding down nine of the top ten rankings and surpassed only by the special telecast of the World Series." In summary, the report stated that "'The Mickey Mouse Club' is completely dominating regular daytime television."

5

DISNEY DAZE

*I don't think we were really aware of how popular
the show was. We were all just kids playing
and having a good time.*

— Mouseketeer SHARON BAIRD

GROOMING THE MOUSEKETEERS FOR STARDOM and creating
their image was the task of the Disney publicity department.
Writing bios and feature stories, scheduling photo sessions, public
appearances, setting up newspaper and magazine interviews, were
among the many promotional activities used to focus the public's
attention on the young performers.

The kids themselves, however, at least during the first season of
filming the show, lived a somewhat sheltered and insular existence on
the Disney Studio lot. While the outside world was singing the prais-
es of "The Mickey Mouse Club" and kids across America were becoming devoted Mouseketeer fans, the young stars themselves were
unaware of their own rapidly growing popularity.

"Doing the show that first year was all-consuming, all-exciting, but none of us really knew the impact we were having," said Tommy Cole. "It really didn't hit us then," added Sharon Baird. "I don't think we realized how important it was until quite a bit later."

Meanwhile, their Disney-issued biographical and feature-story material was distributed to nationwide press with descriptive phrases of each child that echoed the simplicity of the era and was perfect fodder for media placement. For example: "A confident youngster with a vivid imagination and saucy-like looks to match describes Doreen Tracey. Her versatility and pixie manner, augmented by her distinguished bangs and short braided hairdo, plus large wondering eyes, mark her as an outstanding personality."

Darlene Gillespie was described as "a vibrant, freckle-faced youngster with more bounce to the ounce than a bottle of soda pop," while Tommy Cole "is considered a good table tennis player and likes to match abilities with studio personnel. He also plays basketball, enjoys swimming and frequently ice skates. As a hobby, Tommy fills his leisure hours doing leather and copper work."

Bobby Burgess "dances a mile a minute with a smile from ear to ear," and Lonnie Burr "wants an automobile — a custom-made job. That being impractical, he has settled for a bicycle." Annette Funicello, "a well-adjusted girl, is a hobbyist, sports enthusiast and regular church-goer."

Appearing on the TV screen five days a week and being profiled in print on a regular basis, the Mouseketeers not only became idols to America's youngsters but friends to them as well. "The Mouseketeers had a profound influence on my psyche," said Leonard Maltin, a film historian and "Entertainment Tonight" reporter, who, as a child, was a devoted viewer. "You really thought you knew them. I remember I related some of the kids I knew in real life to some of the Mouseketeers. There was one girl in my class in elementary school who was very shy and quiet and so she reminded me of Karen Pendleton.

"But Darlene was my favorite," Maltin continued. "I had a fair-

The Mouseketeers take a milk break at the studio.

ly serious puppy-love crush on her. I can't explain it, it was just that chemical reaction thing. I found her very, very appealing." As for the boy Mouseketeers, Maltin remarked, "I liked Bobby Burgess. He was almost maybe a role model for me. I guess he was what I would have liked to have been like…outgoing, big smile, great personality. And it all seemed so natural."

The kids were, in fact, natural. Basically, what you saw was who they really were. Much of the credit for keeping their toe-tapping feet on the ground was due to the way they were handled at the studio. "The Mouseketeers were treated pretty much like talented kids," explained "Mickey Mouse Club" publicist Leonard Shannon. "Being at Disney, everything was made easy for them but they were not dealt with like stars, which in turn kept them pretty levelheaded."

Another positive influence was the benefit of having their mothers on-site every day. However, the parents didn't spend their time on the set with their kids; instead, they were permanently ensconced in the lobby of the Disney Studio theater.

Tommy Cole explained that "they did let them on the set the very first week, but there were some pushy mamas who were trying to get their kids used more. I think that's when it came down that mothers were not allowed on the set."

"If you had a stage mom, you didn't last on the show," said Bobby Burgess. "I remember one of the girls' mother was being pushy with Mr. Traver, the casting director, and after six months her option was not picked up. Another one tried a different approach. She sat in Mr. Traver's lap! That didn't work either."

"They didn't want stage mothers around," said Virginia Funicello. "So we had to stay in the theater. I was bored to death, so I learned to knit." Knitting seemed to be the pastime of choice for many of the moms. Cubby O'Brien recalled of his mother: "She was a knitter, too, and after the show went off the air, she opened up a knit shop, which she had for many years."

"I remember Cubby's mom knitted all the boys matching sweaters one year," said Bobby. "I even remember what they looked like: they were turtlenecks with blue, red, and white stripes." The young man with the big smile remembers the parents with great appreciation. "Those Mousekemoms sat in that studio theater and that's where they were supposed to be for eight hours a day every day. Now that's a sacrifice."

Not every one of them followed the rules, however. "I used to sneak out and go home so I could cook for my kids, do the wash and iron," confessed Virginia Funicello. "I had two young sons, Michael and Joey, who I had to worry about too." Funicello found a friend and confidant in one of the Disney security guards. "His name was John and he would cover for me," she said. "So if anyone asked 'Where's Mrs. Funicello?' and I wasn't in the theater, then John would call me at home so I could get right back." In typical Italian style, Funicello remarked, "I had a hard time, but at least I could go home and cook a nice meal."

"My life could have been impossible with all those mothers," said producer Bill Walsh. "But they were sort of roped off in one area and they didn't bother me at all. I have an especially happy memory of Mrs. Funicello. She always used to make me a cheesecake — an Italian cheesecake — for Christmas. With ricotta. It was not all bad, believe me."

Annette Funicello and her mother, Virginia, pick up lunch at the studio commissary.

The moms did get to see their kids at lunchtime each day and during breaks when the children would visit the studio theater, sometimes in a rather rambunctious mood. "Cubby and I were in the theater one day and I remember putting gum in his hair," said Karen Pendleton. "I don't know what came over me, but I thought it would

be really funny. He wasn't at all amused and they had to cut it out —
along with a chunk of his hair."

When they did have time to play and have fun, the Mouseketeers
had virtual run of the Disney lot. Twenty-four pairs of strong lungs
audibly signaled their presence regularly throughout the campuslike
studio. As children do everywhere, the Mouseketeers burned up their
youthful energy with a vengeance in impromptu football skirmishes,
tag playing, and ordinary kids' horseplay.

But their playtime was minimal. For the most part they were
either rehearsing, filming, or spending the required three hours a
day at their lessons in the little red schoolhouses. Custom-built, the schoolhouse trailers were parked alongside Soundstage One, the home of "The Mickey Mouse Club." Each seated twenty students with two rows of ten desks on either side of the single room. Typical classroom desks with lift-up tops provided the Mouseketeers' work space. Each child followed an individual daily schedule, all planned by their teacher, Mrs. Jean Seaman, within a master schedule. Although there were several studio teachers on the lot, Mrs. Seaman was the primary tutor for the Mouseketeers.

Mouseketeers rehearse a new dance number.

Residing in the San Fernando Valley, Jean Seaman, a slender woman of medium height with sparkling blue eyes and silver-gray hair, is filled with vitality. Besides working with the Mouseketeers, Mrs. Seaman's teaching career in the Hollywood studio system spanned nearly five decades, during which she tutored such notable child actors as Natalie Wood, when she was just five years old; Jodie Foster, also as a very young child; Ron Howard; Hayley Mills; and, as she remembers, "almost every kid in movies and television from the 1940s through the late '80s"; she retired from teaching in 1988. Her myriad memories also include working with the youngsters who portrayed the von Trapp family in the classic motion picture musical *The Sound of Music*.

The classroom in full swing, with teacher, Mrs. Jean Seaman, in charge.

With a warm smile and quick wit, she delights in talking about "her" Mouseketeers. "Forty-seven subjects were taught in that classroom, including all types of elementary math and French and Spanish at various levels. Our work was planned much like an engineering project in order to get everything in and to allow for interruptions when the children had to work."

Unlike spending continual time in a normal classroom, the Mouseketeers' three-hour requirement was constantly broken up as they were called out when needed on the set. Time

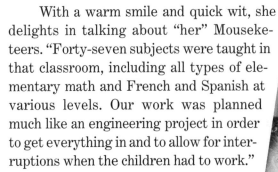

Mrs. Seaman goes over classwork with Mouseketeers Darlene, Doreen, and Bobby while Jimmie Dodd looks on.

Hard at work.

spent in the classroom was accrued in twenty-minute increments to be counted toward the total three-hour requirement. Anything less could not be added to the day's total.

Since pupils ranged in age from eight to fourteen years of age, the curriculum was as individual as the instruction. Each pupil had a personal schedule placed on the wall next to their desk. The schedule was divided into squares that listed the days of the week across the top, with the subjects to be covered in that week along the side of the sheet. As each day's lessons were accomplished, a big X was placed through the appropriate square.

Mrs. Seaman has carefully kept several cardboard boxes filled with the Mouseketeers' essays and compositions, report cards, loose-leaf binders, pencil boxes, and various other school items that chronicled life in the little red schoolhouse. "Those were some of the happiest years of my life," she has said.

At my desk in the front of the room, I had a chart that coincided with theirs. So if anybody had a test or an oral recitation scheduled," she recalled, "I had the information right there in front of me. And I had a chair, a typing chair, that had rollers on it and whenever someone had something to recite, I'd just roll down the aisle."

"Sitting in front of me were Sharon, Doreen, and Annette," said Bobby Burgess. "Now, Sharon was a little whiz in math. Sometimes, in a really low voice, I would whisper, 'Sharon, I'm having a little bit of trouble with this equation — can you do me a favor on this one?'" Mouseketeers or not, they were just like the rest of us.

"Sharon went home at night carrying so many books you couldn't even see her face. And she'd have a handful of pencils sharpened to needlepoints," Karen Pendleton, who sat at a desk at the front of the room, recalled. "I remember Sharon practicing her typing and she would type a mile a minute. And she'd chew gum and it was just so funny because she would chew it as fast as she typed."

Though the kids all had their favorite subjects, the one thing

WALT DISNEY PRODUCTIONS

2400 WEST ALAMEDA AVE. • BURBANK, CALIFORNIA • CABLE ADDRESS: DISNEY

Grades and credits for Annette Funicello - Foreign Language Major

B 9

Subject	Credits	Grade
Algebra I	5	A-
Spanish I	5	A-
English	5	A-
Social Studies	5	A-
Drama	5	B
Physical Education		A

A 9

Subject	Credits	Grade
Algebra II	5	B+
Spanish II	5	B+
English	5	A-
Social Studies	5	B
Typing I	5	A-
Physical Education		A

B 10

	Credits	Grade
Geometry I	5	B+
English	5	B
Life Science & Health I	5	B+
Spanish III	5	A-
Music Appreciation	5	B-
Physical Education	5	A

A 10

	Credits	Grade
Geometry II	5	A-
English	5	B
Life Science & H.II	5	A-
Spanish IV	5	B-
World Affairs	5	A
Physical Education		

B 11

	Credits	Grade
Driver Education	2½	A
American Literature I	5	B
American History I	5	B+
Physiology I	5	B
Spanish V	5	A
Physical Education		

A 11

	Credits	Grade
American Lit. II	5	B-
American History II	5	A-
Physiology II	5	B-
Spanish VI	5	A
Physical Education		

B 12

	Credits	Grade
Senior Composition	5	A
American Government	5	A
World Literature	5	B+
Art Appreciation	5	4
Physical Education		

A 12   *Tentative

	Credits	Grade
Senior Problems	5	
Typing I	5	
Physical Education		

Jean Seaman
Resident Teacher

GR 30461

NO AGREEMENT WILL BE BINDING ON THIS CORPORATION UNLESS IN WRITING AND SIGNED BY AN OFFICER

It wasn't all work as Mrs. Seaman serves up a "Mickey Mouse Club" birthday cake to her young charges.

Annette Funicello's classroom grades.

they nearly all agreed on was how they felt about their teacher. "Mrs. Seaman was brilliant and I love her to this day," said Doreen Tracey. "She was also strict. I would be scared because I have slight dyslexia. Sometimes, when my mind would race, she'd really have to listen to what I was saying because I would jump from subject to subject. But she helped me over a lot of those problems. She really had a very strong role in molding every one of us."

"Oh Doreen, with her big eyelashes flicking," Mrs. Seaman said, smiling. "She had the worst time with spelling. She would say, 'I just don't understand these things!' I helped her get through it."

"Mrs. Seaman taught everything," said Bobby. "And she was great in all subjects. Spanish, math, English, biology, history — everything. And she encouraged us. It made you want to work extra hard, just for her. I know I did. In fact, some of us learned our language lessons so well that we still call each other by our Spanish names. Sharon calls me 'Roberto,' I refer to her as 'Suzita,' and Karen is still 'Chiquita' and Annette 'Anita.'" Mrs. Seaman added, "Bobby always called me 'Señora Océano Hombre'" (Spanish for Mrs. Sea Man!).

Sharon remembers her long-ago teacher as "bright, positive, chipper, and brilliant. She had an answer for every single question that you ever had. And I learned so much from her that when I went back to regular school, I just breezed through with straight A's."

Annette Funicello's loose-leaf binder from her "Mickey Mouse Club" school days

The fondness the Mouseketeers had for their teacher was also reciprocated. "They were great kids," said Mrs. Seaman, "all cooperative, interested, and attentive. I couldn't have accomplished what I did if they weren't. And I wasn't that easy on them either."

"She was tough," said actor Tommy Kirk, who shared the trailer classroom with the Mouseketeers while he was working on "The Hardy Boys," a "Mickey Mouse Club" serial. "She made you work. It wasn't just fun and games. It was a real school. And she used to put a thing on the wall, a weekly lesson plan for every student. Monday, Tuesday, Wednesday, Thursday, Friday; every subject was broken down by things to be accomplished. She was very organized."

"Jean Seaman was one of those wonderful women who inspired you to work your

Musings inside Annette's binder: teenage crushes on Frankie Avalon (whom she would later team up with for a string of Beach Party movies) and heartthrob Fabian.

hardest," said Darlene Gillespie. "I was previously a C student and ended up an A student because of her."

Music Appreciation was a subject Doreen recalled. "Mrs. Seaman decided to assign us all a certain type of music and composer that we had to write a report about," she explained. "For example, for Annette she chose Tchaikovsky because Annette was a ballerina and she loved *Swan Lake*; I believe Bobby was given Joplin, the ragtime composer, and she gave me Strauss. In looking back I realize now that the music and the composer represented our personalities."

Sharon Baird's "Mickey Mouse Club" report card.

The trailer classroom was a place for work but also a place for fun. According to Mrs. Seaman, sometimes the kids' personal habits generated daily chuckles. "The kids would have to lift up the desktop to access things on the inside. All of the Mouseketeers except Darlene would leave their books on the floor when they came in. But every day Darlene would put her books on her desk, sit down, go to get her pencil by lifting up the top of the desk — and crash, all the books would fall on the floor. Everybody waited for it."

She also recollected an idiosyncrasy unique to the dancingest boy Mouseketeer, Bobby. "Bobby used to constantly be moving his feet while sitting at his desk," she said. "Eventually, the studio had to replace the flooring because it was worn through from dancing!"

With children coming and going all day long, books piled under desks, and school projects in various stages of completion, Mrs. Seaman remarked, "I had so much stuff all over the place that one day I

Report card day.

said to the kids, 'Look, I've got to clean this joint up. This is terrible. There is just so much clutter!' And Bobby said, 'Don't, Mrs. Seaman. It's like home.'"

There was one Mouseketeer, however, who didn't feel as fondly about Mrs. Seaman. "I didn't like her as much as everybody else," said Lonnie Burr. "They thought she was wonderful, I didn't. I had problems with her and, as a result, didn't do as well. I actually resorted to cheating on tests and she caught me. It was the first C I ever had in my life; I had always gotten straight A's." Lonnie, who went on to be accepted to college when he was fourteen years old, may not have liked the teacher but ultimately admitted, "I guess I must have learned something."

While Mrs. Seaman was with the Mouseketeers, for the in-and-out three hours a day she had them in her care, she taught with a firm hand and a kind heart. "They were just so eager to learn," she said. "But it wasn't easy with their daily schedule — rehearsals, filming, and school. It really kept them going."

"We may have been different ages," said Doreen, "but the one thing that was predominant among all of us was that we realized we had a responsibility that this was a job and it could lead to other things. We had to conduct ourselves as professionals on that set. Which meant know the dance combinations and learn the routines as fast as we could, because we didn't have time to make mistakes. You had to know your lines and try to do it right the first time. It took strong teamwork, whether you were part of the production team, or a studio teacher, or on the creative side. We all had the same goal."

Because time was of the essence, bad behavior, lateness, or just plain fooling around was not tolerated. "There was no time," Doreen continued. "And that was from the beginning. Dik Darley, our first director, was loved because he was a very quiet, soft-spoken man. You didn't have that pressure coming from Dik, but you could see everyone around him was crazy and nervous because we had so many things to get done. Sometimes I would just think to myself, I'd better get it right or these poor guys are going to have a heart attack if I don't!

Promoted!

That's why kids like Paul Petersen and the Rooney boys just didn't make it."

The reward that came with the hard work was much adulation from the kids on the other side of the television screen who watched every day. And soon the fan mail started to pour in, although it would be some time before the Mouseketeers were really aware of the volume of inquiries about them that was arriving at the studio every day.

"For the first season of the show, we weren't told about our fan mail," said Annette Funicello, who from the very start commanded the lion's share of letters. "But then one day Mr. Disney came to me and jokingly said, 'You must have a lot of Italian relatives because you're getting an awful lot of fan mail.'"

The mail comprised letters of praise, and requests for pictures of the Mouseketeers or individuals such as Walt Disney, Jimmie Dodd, Roy Williams, etc. Gifts ran into the hundreds. Annette recalled receiving "wristwatches, jewelry, and even engagement rings." Since the fan mail acutely reflected the likes and dislikes of the viewing audience, every item of correspondence was read, catalogued, and answered by the Disney fan mail department. As the mail began to surge, arriving from every nook and cranny of the United States, the enthusiasm of young America for the Mouseketeers was growing in leaps and bounds.

The Mouseketeers were also adding to their roster of fans by making public appearances, which they were bound to do as part of their studio contracts. Early on, one of their first such appearances was at Disneyland, under the big top, in "The Mickey Mouse Club Circus."

"We were trained to perform circus acts," explained Sharon Baird. "I remember the girls were Tinker Bell and the boys were Peter Pan. We were in these little green costumes that were kind of fluorescent. I had to climb a rope to the top of the tent, and the lights would go off as the guys would spin me in my glow-in-the-dark cos-

Rehearsals, school, filming, took their toll on the young TV stars.

tume. My mother was more than a little surprised when she first saw me rehearsing up there, and said, 'Sharon, you get down from there this minute!' "

Actually, several of the mothers got into the act themselves. "I was a teddy bear in the circus parade," said Virginia Funicello. "The first night that we performed, my husband didn't know I was in costume. He had taken our two boys out to Disneyland for the weekend, and they were sitting up in the bleachers and I ran up and sat on his lap!"

"My mom was too shy, and didn't participate," said Sharon. "But Tommy's, Bobby's, Doreen's, and Cubby's mothers were among the group that did." The moms played twelve performances and were paid the grand sum of $5.36 per show. It may not have been financially rewarding, but, according to Mrs. Funicello, "It was great fun."

By the end of November 1955, with the show having been on the air seven weeks, an internal memo was sent to casting director Jack Lavin from studio executive Bill Anderson, which stated: "We have reviewed the 24 Mouseketeers now under contract and according to our present production plans we will want to exercise options on the following: Cubby O'Brien, Karen Pendleton, Bobby Burgess, Doreen Tracey, Darlene Gillespie, Annette Funicello, Sharon Baird, Lonnie Burr, Tommy Cole, and Dennis Day. We will let the contracts on the balance of the Mouseketeers expire and either use them on a daily basis or place them under contract at a later date when our production plans for next year are more formally crystallized."

"I was fortunate enough to have my option picked up," recalled Bobby Burgess. "Every six months you always had to be on your toes because that was the time that they could drop you or rehire you. And besides, a little raise went along with that and you smiled a lot around Mr. Disney."

"We knew we were replaceable," said Tommy Cole. "We were the envy of every child in America and their parents too. But there were thousands of kids waiting for our job if we didn't measure up."

In April 1956 the search began for new Mouseketeers to replace those who had been dropped. This time, riding on the coattails of "The Mickey Mouse Club"'s first-season success, a media and promotional blitz from the Disney Studio kicked off the launch of a national talent search.

6
MARKETING MADNESS

Walt's Profit Formula:
Dream, Diversify and Never Miss an Angle.

— *The Wall Street Journal*, headline Disney story,
February 4, 1958

RESPONDING TO A FLOOD OF MAIL from kids all over the country requesting information on how they could appear on "The Mickey Mouse Club," Walt Disney Productions, ABC-TV, and leading department stores across the nation joined forces in mid-April, 1956, to conduct a National Talent Round-Up. The search would seek talented youngsters to appear as guests on the show, as well as children who displayed exceptional talent, to join the ranks of the second-season contingent of Mouseketeers.

Capitalizing on the success of the show, the National Talent Round-Up represented a tremendous opportunity to generate publicity for "The Mickey Mouse Club" in major cities across the United

States. ABC drafted their local affiliate stations across the country into service to promote the talent search locally on TV while the ABC Radio Network dispatched the message through local radio. Adding to the publicity buildup were ads placed in local newspapers announcing the Talent Round-Up.

Expanding upon these resources, large department stores in twelve selected cities (New York City; Newark; Boston; Philadelphia; Washington, D.C.; Cincinnati; Cleveland; Grand Rapids and Lansing, Michigan; Oklahoma City; San Francisco; and Los Angeles) also participated in the promotion, with one store in each city billed as the "Official 'Mickey Mouse Club' Talent Round-Up Headquarters." Boys and girls between the ages of five and fourteen were invited to come into the store to fill out entry blanks (amidst elaborate product displays, featuring a diverse variety of "Mickey Mouse Club" and Disney character merchandise). Later, auditions were scheduled — either in the store or in public schools or local theaters. Every child who showed up for an audition received an impressive Certificate of Talent provided by Walt Disney Productions.

From this initial screening, each store chose a group of local winners who received merchandise prizes (provided by Disney-licensed manufacturers) and a screen test. Walt Disney Productions then arranged for professional camera and recording technicians to film each local winner in his own city. These films were then flown to the West Coast for further study by a casting committee headed by Walt Disney.

Approximately four final winners were chosen from each group of local winners. Each received a free round-trip flight to California with a parent or guardian, a guest appearance on "The Mickey Mouse

Talent Award presented to children who participated in local TV station and department-store auditions for "The Mickey Mouse Club."

Club" TV program, two days of fun at Disneyland, luxury accommodations, and a sightseeing tour of Hollywood.

From the various Talent Round-Up auditions around the country, plus those held at the Disney Studio, numerous youngsters were chosen to appear as guests on "The Mickey Mouse Club." Seven children were selected to become new Mouseketeers: Sherry Alberoni, Eileen Diamond, Cheryl Holdridge, Charley Laney, Larry Larsen,

Jay-Jay Solari, and Margene Storey. Except for Cheryl Holdridge, who would remain a Mouseketeer until 1959, the end of the series, each of the others appeared on the show during its second (1956–57) season only.

"My brother was the one who originally got the audition for 'The Mickey Mouse Club,'" explained Sherry Alberoni. "But he was a drummer and they already had Cubby. When they asked him if he played any other instrument, he said, 'No, but I have a little sister who tap-dances.'" Ten-year-old Sherry auditioned for, among others, Sidney Miller, who took over "The Mickey Mouse Club" director reins in 1956. "I had a lisp," she said, "and Sid Miller thought it was hysterical; he loved it. I guess it came in handy, because it helped get me hired.

Miller, a show-business veteran and onetime child star, had worked as an actor at MGM during its heyday with such entertainment notables as Judy Garland, Mickey Rooney, and Jackie Cooper. He appeared in numerous films and went on to live stage work, as well as appearing on television variety shows, writing for TV, and, eventually, directing.

In addition to Sherry Alberoni, Miller's new additions to the Mouseketeer roster each brought special talents to the show. Eileen Diamond specialized in modern dance and ballet; blonde, blue-eyed Cheryl Holdridge was a gifted all-around performer; Charley Laney, an accomplished dancer and gymnast; Larry

Roy Alberoni, Mouseketeer Sherry Alberoni's brother, who originally auditioned for the show but didn't get chosen.

Director Sid Miller gives instructions to Jimmie and the Mouseketeers.

SID MILLER

80

Larsen, an expert tap dancer; Jay-Jay Solari, a versatile dancer with tap a specialty; and dark-haired, dark-eyed Margene Storey, a skillful dancer.

Among those who became Mouseketeers in 1956: Eileen Diamond, Cheryl Holdridge, Charley Laney, Larry Larsen, Sherry Alberoni, and Margene Storey.

MARGENE

EILEEN

SHERRY

CHERYL

CHARLEY

LARRY

"We auditioned kids all over the country and actually we ran across many kids who had as much or even more talent than our established group of Mouseketeers," said Sid Miller. "But we were looking for something more than talent, we were searching for personality as well." Accustomed to the ways of child performers, Miller explained, "In the old days, the moppets in makeup were hardened vets. For many of them, their parents were in show business. The kids knew all the studio gossip, could understand the subtleties of the small print in a contract, and, above all, were frankly aware of their importance."

The Mouseketeers, on the other hand, were quite different. "They were mainly children of non-pros," he said. "They had great talent, too, but their attitude was different. Another thing we didn't have on 'The Mickey Mouse Club' was the Professional Mother. When I was a kid, the mamas used to sit on the sidelines all day long and interfere with production and generally get into everybody's hair. The mothers would almost cut each other's throats trying to push their little ones into the limelight. At Disney, they were not permitted on the set. They'd bring their children to the studio, then spend the rest of the day in the theater knitting or playing cards. It was delightful."

The Mouseketeers, who had only worked with first-season director Dik Darley, an easygoing, soft-spoken man, had to adjust to a very different style with taskmaster Miller. "He was a tyrant," said Lonnie Burr. "He terrified me. I was always there on time, always knew my lines, I was professional. But if you were waiting for a shot and would talk, he'd say, 'Shut up, don't talk!' "

Conversely, Miller's opinion of the young Burr was also not without criticism. "He was very ambitious," said Miller. "He made a point of impressing people. Just his drive and his 'I want to get this and I want to get that.' He was a climbing kid." According to the director, his method of working with the Mouseketeers was not to make their job more difficult but "to get the best out of them as kids, as human beings and real people. You know, not overstepping their age bounds.

They loved what they were doing," he said. "They were cooperative and would try something, even if they didn't feel comfortable with it."

"I always thought Sid Miller was funny," said Mouseketeer drummer Cubby O'Brien. "I mean, if he'd get mad at us I'd never take him seriously. He'd make me laugh because sometimes he would just get so frustrated with us that he'd get down on his knees and plead, 'Please, please, get this take! We've done it twelve times!' He'd just lose it sometimes."

Sid Miller and Mouseketeers on the set.

Tommy Cole said, "He was the only director that ever made me cry." The tears were the result of Sid's berating the young performer. "I didn't know the words to something," Tommy explained. "I had just gotten the lyrics that morning and hadn't had time to learn them. At any rate, he yelled at me in front of a lot of other people. It really upset and embarrassed me." The director, however, quickly realized his blunder and apologized to Cole.

With the second-year team in place, "The Mickey Mouse Club" embarked upon its most successful season and the one in which the Mouseketeers would get their first real taste and understanding of their enormous success. It was also the year in which "Mickey Mouse Club" merchandise sales would soar. By far the most popular selling item was the replica of the Mouseketeers' mouse-eared cap.

"The black felt beanie with the big round plastic ears must be one of the most popular souvenirs in the galaxy," reported *Travel & Leisure* in a March 1990 article. "Following the premiere of 'The Mickey Mouse Club' in 1955, the popular hat quickly became one of the definitive fads of an era that spawned the Davy Crockett coonskin cap, the Barbie doll and the Hula Hoop. An early advertisement from the Benay-Albee Novelty Company of Maspeth, New York — which manufactured the hats — exhorted retailers: 'Cash in on this fast-selling Mickey Mouse beanie! Twenty-five-million kids see it worn daily on Disney's Mouseketeer TV program, coast-to-coast. It's by far the fastest selling novelty hat today!' "

The first commercial hats had only an *M* on the front and the market was soon flooded with imitations. Disney quickly changed the medallion to include the word *Mouseketeers* and the image of Mickey Mouse — trademarked logos. The competition soon disappeared. The original all-black version of the ears sold for 69¢ and after "The Mickey Mouse Club" had been on the air only twelve weeks, over 2,000,000 hats had been sold.

MERCHANDISE

By February 1956 thirty-eight companies had designed, created, promoted, and were selling "Mickey Mouse Club" character merchandise. Besides the Mouseketeer hats, some of the most popular selling items were T-shirts, records, record players, balloons, Mousegetars (toy replicas of Jimmie Dodd's on-screen guitar), play outfits, sleepwear, jackets, socks, belts, suspenders, shoes, books, games, puzzles, and inflatable vinyl toys.

Prices for such merchandise varied, but by today's standards, items were quite inexpensive. In selected ads, for example:

"The Mickey Mouse Club Portable Phonograph comes complete with the Mickey Mouse Club March and Song Record, and a package of needles. The phonograph bears a lifetime guarantee. The phonograph features a red and white striped lid which closes over a solid blue base. A Mickey Mouse Club emblem is on the inner lid. Retail price: $12.95."

"Mickey Mouse Club Bubble Bath Set contains one Mickey Mouse modeled in castile soap and one container of scented bubble bath. Retailing for 69¢, it is packaged in a black, white and red box which features Disney characters."

"Mickey Mouse guitar plays real music. The Mousegetar has nylon strings, tuning keys, pick and carrying cord. Mickey Mouse's face decorates the bright red musical instrument. Jimmie Dodd's instruction book, which teaches the Mickey Mouse Club songs easily, is included. Individually packaged in a carrying case. Retail price: $4.00."

New, Colorful SUPER-SELLING Toys Featuring...

the mickey mouse club "Mousekateers"

...The Youngsters' Favorite TV Show!

"MOUSEKATEER" PADDLE AND BALL GAME!

Large deluxe paddle in

MOUSEKAPADDLE

Backed by national promotion and advertising.

OFFICIAL MICKEY MOUSE CLUB RETURNING "MOUSEKATOP"

High Quality Beginner's Model. Sturdy construction, beautiful finish.

#608—Packed two dozen assorted colors in attractive counter top display carton. Six cartons to a master. Shipping weight, 15 lbs.

JIMMY DODD PROFESSIONAL MODEL RETURNING "MOUSEKATOP"

• Balanced
• Free Wheeling
• Highest Quality

#607—Packed two dozen assorted colors in attractive counter top display carton. Six cartons to master. Shipping weight, 18 lbs.

MICKEY MOUSE CLUB ROUND-UP
COWBOY BELT and BOLO TIE

FINEST LEATHER ... BY Chambers   PHOENIX

MICKEY MOUSE CLUB

ADMIRAL
toy corporation
5555 west peterson avenue ● chicago 45, illinois.

HERE'S YOUR OFFICIAL JIMMIE DODD Returning MOUSEKATOP

© Walt Disney Productions

"Walt Disney's official Mouseketeer Doll, 12" tall, is molded of soft lifelike vinyl plastic with emphasis on detail; her panties, shoes, socks, sweater and hat are molded as an integral part of the doll and spray painted in contrasting colors to her reddish brown molded hair and flesh colored skin. She wears a cute cotton skirt which is removable and flares out to give the effect of twirling motion; the skirts are made in a variety of colors. Her hat is identical to that worn by real Mouseketeers and has a little painted bow centered between two black mouse ears. Her sweater has the Mickey Mouse Club insignia in relief, with the face of Mickey Mouse in black on a white background. She has jointed arms and legs and her head can be turned from one side to the other; she can be made to sit or stand in a variety of positions. Retail: $2.98."

ANNOUNCING.

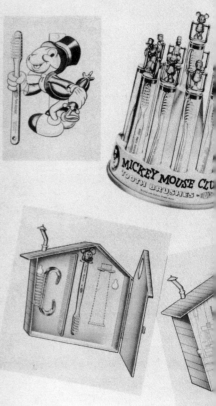

MICKEY MOUSE CLUB TOOTH BRUSHES

THE OFFICIAL MICKEY MOUSE CLUB TV BULB AND NITE-LITE

Inspired by Walt Disney's MICKEY MOUSE CLUB TV Show

A Product of Solar Electric Corporation

Retail price: 89c

Sturdily constructed with medium skirted brass base. Screws into any table or floor lamp socket. Heavy duty glass — featuring MICKEY MOUSE design. Economical low wattage 5,000 hour filament. Has SOLAR'S special "Eyease" white coating. Prevents glare and hotspots on TV screen. Restful to the eye. Ideal for nursery night light. Bulb never gets hot. Can be handled while burning. Cutout of MICKEY MOUSE in Band Leader's uniform on back of colorful window package. Legs fit on bulb adding novelty touch.

The studio gave the merchandisers great promotional support. Posters, streamers, banners, logos, insignia, emblems, etc., designed in the company's New York and California offices, were distributed and used freely by participating companies. All the general information about Walt Disney Productions or "The Mickey Mouse Club" that would help licensees or sponsors outside the Disney company was made available and even adapted to their particular need on request.

ive Line of Products
PONT using the Famous
t Disney Fanciful Characters

MICKEY MOUSE CLUB
OFFICIAL
TOOTH BRUSHES by DU PONT

MICKEY MOUSE CLUB
OFFICIAL
COMBS FOR BOYS AND GIRLS by DU PONT

BE ON THE LOOKOUT
FOR full details and illustrations of this line of products.
DU PONT will send this information to you shortly.

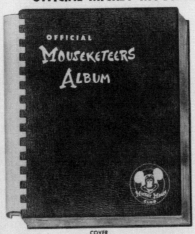

OFFICIAL MICKEY MOUSE CLUB ALBUM RESULT IN PROFITABLE SALES

OFFICIAL
MOUSEKETEERS ALBUM

COVER

12 INSIDE PAGES IN COLOR

First innovation in Photo Albums in 50 Years — A Novel Color-illustrated Mickey Mouse Foto-Biography Album. Exciting fun for children who can paste their favorite snapshots alongside MICKEY MOUSE, PLUTO, ETC. 12 Colorful Pages.

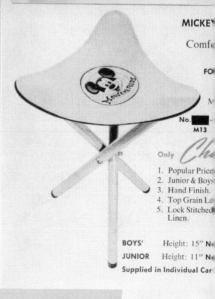

WALT DISNEY PRODUCTIONS, INC. · CHARACTER MERCHANDISING DIVISION · 477 MADISON AVE., NEW YORK 22, N. Y.

A WALT DISNEY

HUSTLEGRAM

BE THE FIRST TO SELL

OFFICIAL MICKEY MOUSE CLUB COASTER WAGONS AND SCOOTER

"THE MOUSEKETEER EXPRESS!"

Bright orange wagon showing Pluto dashing away with wagon and Mickey Mouse trying to stop him. White wheels striped in orange to match body. Large semi pneumatic tires. Congo Graphite Bearings for super speed! (Body size 34" x 15½" x 4") Same model available with larger wheels.

"THE MOUSEKETEER COASTER!"

Brilliant turquoise blue body has Donald Duck pulling Huey and Dewey in a wagon as fast as they can with Louie trailing. Sparkling white wheels.

(Body size 24" x 12" x 3¼".)

"THE MEESEKETEER* SCOOTER!"

The large Mouseketeer emblem on the front of this streamline little scooter immediately identifies a Meeseketeer.* There's an extra foot rest for feet. Color: red.

(Frame 24" length, 25" height. Bright gray wheels 5" x ½".)

*Very little boy or very little girl

Today original "Mickey Mouse Club" products are much sought after on the collector's market.
"The merchandise was incredible," said Annette Funicello. "There were dolls and books and bracelets and all kinds of jewelry. I wish I had thought to save that stuff, but who ever dreamed it would be worth anything?"

"Mickey Mouse Club" promotions with grocery products.

The merchandise explosion was supported by large-scale "Mickey Mouse Club" marketing campaigns from both the Disney Studio and ABC television. One of the more unique ways in which they worked to capture additional exposure for the show was the use of Pitney Bowes postage-meter plates. In February 1956 the ABC network made available to all of their "Mickey Mouse Club" stations across the country, free of charge, Pitney Bowes postage-meter plates that imprinted " 'Mickey Mouse Club' on ABC-TV, Monday thru Friday, 5–6 p.m.," on all outgoing mail. These miniature "billboards" on literally hundreds of thousands of pieces of mail provided tremendous exposure for the show.

Another ingenious marketing concept, jointly initiated by Disney and ABC, was to bring the "Disneyland" show and "The Mickey Mouse Club" directly into the classroom in schools across the nation by creating the *Disney on Television Classroom Guide*, a twelve-page, illustrated booklet designed to be a teacher's guide and emphasizing the educational aspects of the Disney programs. More than 300,000 *Guides* were distributed to schools. The project in itself served to bring "The Mickey Mouse Club" to the attention of an estimated 10,000,000 school children.

Utilizing various Disney divisions to participate in as many cross-promotional opportunities as possible to further support "The Mickey Mouse Club" reflected Walt Disney's marketing genius. In 1958, a *Wall Street Journal* article entitled "Walt's Profit Formula: Dream, Diversify and Never Miss an Angle," illustrated the Disney company's successful use of "integration" — or "synergy," as it's referred to today — as an important and beneficial marketing tool.

The article reported that "Walter E. Disney and his crew of starry-eyed artists and ingenious innovators are kings of the kid frontier...but they're also shrewd businessmen. Stated Roy Disney, president of Walt Disney Productions and older brother of Chairman Walt, 'our profitable record is based on the fact that our diversified activities are related and tend to complement each other. Integration is the key word around here; we don't do anything in one line without giving a thought to its likely profitability in our other lines.'"

The article also stated, "Television has given a big boost to Disney's merchandise-licensing activities. The best-selling Disney item to date is the Mouseketeer's hat that is part of the get-up worn by youngsters on 'The Mickey Mouse Club.'"

The roots of Disney synergy actually go back over six decades to 1929 when a stranger walked up to Walt Disney in a hotel lobby and offered him $300 to put Mickey Mouse's likeness on a children's pencil tablet he was manufacturing. Walt, needing the money, accepted, launching Disney licensing.

Just a year later, in 1930, a daily Mickey Mouse comic strip began appearing in newspapers and the first Disney book, entitled *The Mickey Mouse Book*, was published. As Mickey gained popularity, so did Disney synergy, with licensed merchandise helping to promote the new animated character to international fame.

Licensing also proved enormously successful for the company in 1937 with the release of *Snow White and the Seven Dwarfs*. It was one of the first films in motion picture history to have an entire merchandising and promotional campaign in place by opening day.

In the years that followed, the company gained tremendous success through its motion picture and licensing efforts, which continued to grow as did the cross-promotional opportunities within the corporation. But perhaps the most significant milestone in Disney synergy history came with the advent of television.

While broadcasting the first Disney TV show, "One Hour in Wonderland," in 1950, Walt Disney quickly realized the potential of the medium to cross-promote his films. Even more significant in the next few years was Walt's use of his weekly TV show to generate awareness and excitement among millions of viewers for his newest venture, Disneyland. By using synergy with the power of television, Walt was able to pre-sell his new theme park to an entire generation of Americans before the gates ever opened.

Disneyland itself then became a premier showcase for Disney synergy efforts through the use of attractions and displays that promoted Disney films and television shows, the sale of licensed merchandise, and appearances in-park by Disney celebrities such as the Mouseketeers. Each link in the Disney chain helped support the other, and, in turn, increased the level of success for the entire company.

Using these techniques to their best advantage in relation to "The Mickey Mouse Club," Disney's studio publications staff came up with yet another promotional vehicle for the show, *Walt Disney's Mickey Mouse Club Magazine*. A plan was initiated in the summer of 1955, and by November the color, subscription-based quarterly magazine was launched and being promoted by Jimmie Dodd on the daily show. Subscriptions were priced at $1.00 per year, and were mailed directly to subscribers from the printing company. Each subscriber received an official "Mickey Mouse Club" Membership Certificate and Identification Card. The magazine was entirely staffed by Disney writers and illustrated by significant Disney artists of the period.

Walt Disney's Mickey Mouse Club Magazine's first cover.

In addition to viewers of the show being able to order the magazine by mail, Disney's Character Merchandising Division worked with selected department stores across the country to establish their outlet as the Official Headquarters for *Walt Disney's Mickey Mouse Club Magazine* subscriptions in their town. Offering stores this opportunity would allow them to bring more traffic into their establishments while Disney would benefit with added local promotion for the new publication. The lure for the kids to go to the department store and subscribe rather than mail in their subscriptions was the instant availability of the official Membership Certificates and Identification Cards. As of early February, 1956 there were approximately 195,000 subscribers to *Walt Disney's Mickey Mouse Club Magazine*.

The cover of the 42-page first issue featured twelve Mouseketeers, along with Jimmie Dodd and Roy Williams, each decked out in their western Talent Round-Up costumes. The opening page featured a message from Walt Disney: *"The Mickey Mouse Club Magazine is dedicated to the leaders of the twenty-first century, some of whom are among you Mouseketeers of today. The skills and arts and sciences which you are developing will help fashion a better world for tomorrow. Every one of us has some talent, and talent is developed by doing. This is the theme of our television show — and of this magazine as well. We want to encourage your contributions and comments and criticism, as these will help us in making the magazine more truly yours."*

Some of the stories contained in the issue included: "Meet the Mouseketeers," "Animal Autobiographies: The Story of the Buffalo," "Spin and Marty," "I'm No Fool on a Bicycle," by Jiminy Cricket, "Disneyland's Snow White Ride," "Davy Crockett's Almanac," "The Mickey Mouse Club Circus," and, in his own words, "The Story of My Life," by Mickey Mouse.

THE STORY OF MY LIFE

by

MICKEY MOUSE

"Hi, folks! Guess we don't need any introductions. Y'know — it's really a tough job writing the story of your life without making yourself sound important... especially if you've done as much as *I* have...ooop!...there I go! Well, anyway, it seems the whole thing started on a train. That must have been twenty-five years ago.

"Y'see Walt was coming back to Hollywood to try something new in cartoons, 'cause the business was getting into a rut. The public was fed up with cartoon rabbits...and cats and things...they wanted new faces.

"So what does Walt do? He remembers he had a pet mouse when he was a boy...and so...he decides to make a star out of something that looks like a *mouse*. Turned out to be *me!*...The *new face!* Now I never was one of those cute soft little mice that lived in the woodwork and raided mousetraps. I was a *character*...right from the start. Y'see, Walt and I fixed it so I could ride a bicycle, play a trombone, drive a car and all that stuff, right from the start...see?

"First picture we made I imitated Charles Lindbergh and built my own plane. 'Course I never got to Paris...heh!...never even got out of the barnyard. That home-made crate wasn't fast...but it was noisy...while it lasted. Say — I almost forgot. Minnie...(she's my girl)...played in that picture, too.

"Walt kinda surprised me by finding me a girlfriend right from the start. And what a girl! I call her the 'Mouse Beautiful.' Except for the three or four fights we have every week, Minnie an' I get along like a couple of love-birds.

"Well — so much for sentiment — let's get back to my career. Inside of a few months I played a Gaucho (remember those ten-gallon pants?) — then I was a riverboat captain...a brave engineer...owner of an opry house, an' even a dancing fool. No matter what kind of a part Walt and I cooked up together, I put everything I had into it. Slowly we climbed the ladder of success side by side. It was a lot easier now, 'cause I was wearing shoes. And I'd learned a lot of new tricks about make-up. But no matter how my looks improved I never got a swelled head…not me.

"Fame an' fortune doesn't come easy, you know…you've got to fight every step of the way. One of the biggest headaches was a crude person named Pete. Minnie described him in two words… *im-possible*. Sometimes I think Walt invented him just to see if I was really indestructible. Why, I saved Minnie from Pete's clutches so often it got to be a habit. It was almost a relief when Walt let me tangle with a gorilla for a change.

"Another time I got messed up with a giant about the size of the Empire State Building and even though I was lucky and came out on top, I wouldn't care for giants as a steady diet. But some good things happened too…I found myself with a pet named Pluto. He was a loose-jointed pooch with built-in fleas, but he had a heart of gold. Just between us, I think Minnie was just a *little* bit jealous of him.

"As the seasons went by, Walt and I built up quite a cast. There was Clarabelle Cow, Horace Horsecollar, the operatic Clara Cluck, and good old fun-loving Goofy with the satchel feet and the foghorn voice. But as the poet says, 'into each life some rain must fall.' And this time it came down in buckets…for who showed up but *Donald Duck*. A noisy little gent with chips on both shoulders. He never had to look for trouble 'cause trouble looked for Donald. But just as we were getting used to our little feathered friend, something *good* happened. We had a chance to perform in *color!*

"To celebrate this event we put on a super-duper band concert, using the whole company. Of course Donald showed up and tried his best to mess things up. And just as we got *him* settled down, a cyclone blew in…and we took off for outer space. But I'll say one thing for our band…even though we were spread all over the landscape, we never missed a note. Oh, we found a way to put Donald in his place, too. All we did was hire a crowd of innocent-looking orphans. They looked like little angels, but every time they met up with Donald they ran him ragged. And just for variety we put in our second team now and then…a pair of chipmunks…and poor old Donald hasn't relaxed in years.

"As the seasons rolled by, the one thing that seemed to send all of us was music. We started working banjos, brass an' drums into our cartoons…then we found ourselves going all out for Hawaiian tunes, South American Sambas, Chinese, Arabian, Eskimo, and a few choice hunks of grand opera. The musical background was a great break for me when Leopold Stokowski stepped into the picture.

"The famous conductor not only featured me in 'Fantasia' playing the lead in the big 'Sorcerer' number, but insisted that I appear with him as a guest conductor! The way he called me up to the podium, shook hands and bowed to me would have swelled many a mouse's head — but not *mine!* I realized Mister Stokowski had worked just as hard as I had — and deserved just as much credit. You could hardly blame me for getting a little bit sentimental when I remembered this big opening took place at the Broadway Theater in New York — the same place I first appeared as a ragged, shoeless mouse, only ten years before!

"During the past year or so there has been a lot of feverish activity around the studio — and a whole flock of new faces. The excitement started almost like a whisper…'t.v.' — 'T.V.' — 'T! V!' Pretty soon we found out it meant that a lot of folks would see us on their television sets as well as in the theaters. It finally built up into something you all know about, 'The Mickey Mouse Club.'

"Boy, you could have knocked me over with a kilocycle when I heard that Walt expected me to open the program day after day and say 'Hello' to all of you in person. It's just like shaking hands with a million old friends — and looking forward to meeting a few million new ones. Wow! If anyone could write a life story with a happier ending than this one, he'll have to show *me!* So Hi, Everybody! — And here's looking forward to a lot of fun for a long time to come!"

ULTIMATELY, *Walt Disney's Mickey Mouse Club Magazine* reached a peak circulation of 400,000, which kept many young Mouseketeers faithful to their favorite daily television show. A questionnaire, based on the contents of the first issue, was mailed to 1,000 subscribers incorporating all the United States and evenly divided between large cities and small towns or rural areas. Based on their responses, it was found that the average age of readers was 9½ and their favorite article in the issue was "Meet the Mouseketeers."

The Mouseketeers, in fact, also scored first on articles subscribers would like more of, as well as number one on what they liked best about "The Mickey Mouse Club" television show. From a list of the nine core-group Mouseketeers, readers were asked to indicate their favorites. In popularity order, the question produced the following results: Annette, Karen, Cubby, Darlene, Bobby, Doreen, Sharon, Tommy, and Lonnie.

Dragging up the rear, Lonnie may have been the least favorite among this particular group of kids questioned; however, he was first in the heart of the number one Mouseketeer. "I had a crush on Lonnie," said Annette. "He was actually the first big crush that I ever had. And I also gave him my first kiss. I thought he was just so cool."

After working, playing, and going to school together every day for many months during the first two seasons of "Mickey Mouse Club" production, the Mouseketeers were no longer just a group of talented kids who spent time together; they were childhood chums whose friendships would intrinsically connect them for life.

7
THE SERIALS

Nothing I have ever done and possibly nothing I will ever accomplish in the future could touch as many lives and bring pleasure to as many people as did "The Mickey Mouse Club."

— TIM CONSIDINE,
star of "Spin and Marty" and "The Hardy Boys"

AN ENORMOUS AMOUNT OF FAN MAIL was also coming in that was directed to the young stars of what could be called television's first mini-series, "Spin and Marty." Making its debut on "The Mickey Mouse Club" on November 11, 1955, the serialized story was based on the book *Marty Markham*, by Lawrence Edward Watkin. Originally, the serial was to be centered around the character of Marty, and a casting call went out to find a young boy to fill the role. "I auditioned for the part of Marty and got it," said actor Tim Considine, although he would eventually play the role of Spin.

Fifteen-year-old Considine was the son of movie producer John Considine and the nephew of Bob Considine, well-known newspaper writer. His mother, Carmen Pantages, was a member of the eminent theatrical family. An acting veteran, Tim came to the Disney Studio having appeared in a number of films, including *The Clown*, with Red Skelton; *Her Twelve Men*, with Greer Garson; and *The Private War of Major Benson*, with Charlton Heston. After auditioning for "Spin and Marty," the acting veteran knew exactly what he wanted.

David Stollery (left) portrayed Marty and Tim Considine (right) Spin in the popular "Mickey Mouse Club" serial "Spin and Marty."

"In reading the part, I decided I didn't want to be that snotty kid Marty," Tim recalled. "I wanted to be Spin, the really cool guy who was his friend, but that role was a really small part." But even at his tender age the teenager knew what was right for him and argued with his agent about the role. After Tim's agent discussed the situation with Bill Walsh and the rest of the creative team, it was decided to rewrite the whole story to build up the role of Spin and make the two roles more equal. "And that," said Tim, "is how it became 'Spin and Marty.'"

Considine also recollects that he may have been the one to recommend young actor David Stollery to Disney to fill the role of Marty. "I had worked with David on *Her Twelve Men* and we became friends. I just thought he would be perfect in the role and I seem to remember suggesting him to Disney," said Considine. David was brought in, screen tested, and he won the role of Marty.

Tim and David were cast as the hero and the villain, respectively, of the "Spin and Marty" series, which followed the exploits of a group of boys who spend their summer vacation at the Triple R Ranch. Tim portrayed Spin, the good-humored youngster who tries hard to help the other boys get acclimated to life on a ranch. David portrayed Marty Markham, the rich city boy who doesn't like ranches, and makes life difficult for the other youngsters in the process.

Location filming for the production took place at the Golden Oak Ranch near Newhall, California, about twenty-seven miles from the studio in Burbank. Work on the 25-episode series began on June 28, 1955, with both Tim and David earning $400 per week in salary. The budget for "Spin and Marty" was a hefty $513,480, and would eventually come in at $573,000, about $60,000 over budget because of a Screen Actors Guild strike that took place midway through production.

Although "Spin and Marty" was a key segment on the new "Mickey Mouse Club," since it was filmed outside the studio and all episodes had been completed by September 1955, before "The Mickey Mouse Club" debuted, young Tim Considine had no idea the serial was part of a bigger show. "We didn't know what the hell 'The Mickey Mouse Club' was," admitted Considine. "We were just doing a show out there on the ranch. But one day I had to be at the studio for something or other and I remember walking out of the commissary and seeing these little kids. They were wearing cream-colored shirts with their names on them and blue skirts and pants and they had on these hats that I once described as a yarmulke with wings. I was fascinated."

Considine's fascination led him to follow the group of youngsters back to the soundstage on which they were working. "I watched amazed as they sang and danced," he said. "The first thing I thought was I'm glad that I don't have to do that, because singing and dancing in front of cameras was an entirely different thing than acting. I was just so relieved that it wasn't me. At any rate, that was the first time I realized what 'The Mickey Mouse Club' and the Mouseketeers were and that 'Spin and Marty' was a part of something much larger than a series by itself."

"Spin and Marty" catapulted Considine in particular into the limelight where he soon became an idol to millions of young Mickey Mouse Club followers, as well as popular with a good segment of the adult population. Typical of the thousands of letters received was the following, addressed to Walt Disney: "After our family enjoyed every minute of your great Davy Crockett stories, I thought you would never top them or even duplicate them. But here you go again — with your 'Spin and Marty' series on 'The Mickey Mouse Club' show. My six-year-old son is enthralled with the horses — my almost thirteen-year-old girl is in love with Spin and Marty and my husband and I love the whole show. You are to be congratulated a million times for your wonderful, clean, wholesome shows for the whole family."

For Considine, the admiration was somewhat intimidating.

"Because I'm a very private person and was even more so back then as well as being bashful, I was amazed at Spin's popularity and was not terribly comfortable with it. I had never experienced anything like that kind of notoriety and I really wasn't ready for it. It was way over the top."

Motivated by the receipt of some 30,000 fan letters pleading for more chapters into life on the Triple R Ranch, a second season's "Further Adventures of Spin and Marty" (which also starred Annette Funicello and cherub-faced Kevin Corcoran as "Moochie") was pro-

Annette Funicello appeared on "The Further Adventures of Spin and Marty."

duced, along with a third, "The New Adventures of Spin and Marty," in 1957. Annette returned to the final series and Mouseketeer Darlene Gillespie was also added to that cast.

Darlene was given the opportunity to star in her own serial, "Corky and White Shadow," during the first season of "The Mickey Mouse Club." Portraying Corky Brady, she headlined along with Buddy Ebsen (co-star of Disney's "Davy Crock-

Annette and Darlene both joined the cast of "The New Adventures of Spin and Marty."

Darlene portrayed Corky in her own serial, "Corky and White Shadow."

ett") and a white German shepherd, named Harvey, as White Shadow. The 17-episode serial introduced a female teenage heroine to the nation's youngsters.

As described in George W. Woolery's book *Children's Television: The First Thirty-five Years*, "The setting was Glen Forks, a small southwestern town, where Corky lived with her father, Sheriff Matt Brady, played by Buddy Ebsen. After a local bank was robbed by the notorious Durango Dude and Eddie, the sheriff organized a posse and gave chase. Wounding the gunmen in the ensuing shoot-out, Brady captured Eddie, but Durango eluded the posse. Meanwhile, Corky and White Shadow, on an outing in the woods, stopped by to visit her Uncle Dan at his cabin. When she stumbled across the wounded Durango in the woods, Corky sent White Shadow for her father, but when the sheriff arrived, the Dude threatened the girl's life and Brady backed off.

The outlaw tied Corky to a tree but their location was disclosed when he shot a poisonous snake endangering the girl. Captured and placed behind bars, Durango was freed by Eddie, who had managed to escape. They hid out at Dan's cabin, holding him hostage. Searching for her missing dog, Corky and her friend Freddy spotted the crook's hideout and alerted the sheriff. Corky and Freddy then found White Shadow living happily in a nearby canyon with his pups and a mother coyote."

A number of songs were incorporated into the plot to showcase young Gillespie's singing talents. Although the serial placed her in her own special spotlight, Darlene was not particularly enamored of the role and some twenty years later, according to Woolery's book, referred to the series as "horrendous."

Other serials incorporated into the 1955 "Mickey Mouse Club" included "What I Want to Be," filmed at TWA headquarters in Kansas City, depicting special training procedures for becoming an airline stewardess and a pilot; "Foreign Correspondent," covering stories focusing on places and events in England, Japan, Mexico, and Italy; the "Let's Go" series, exploring skin diving, shark hunting, and an elephant round-up; "Christmas 'Round the World" as celebrated in Switzerland, Holland, Mexico, Denmark, and Sweden; and "Animal Autobiographies."

Another popular serial that debuted in 1956 was "The Hardy Boys," starring Tim Considine (the ever-popular Spin) as Frank Hardy and "Mickey Mouse Club" newcomer Tommy Kirk as Joe Hardy, the two sons of a famous private detective. Aired in twenty installment episodes, the serial, set in Bayport, U.S.A., concerned the efforts of Frank and Joe Hardy to rival their detective father, Fenton, by trying to find

lost pirate riches (in "The Mystery of the Applegate Treasure") reputedly handed down from generation to generation in the Applegate family.

The story unfolds as we learn that an earlier search for the treasure proved futile, and by the time the Hardy boys come on the scene, there is a great deal of doubt among the townspeople that the treasure ever existed except in old man Applegate's imagination. All this is quickly dispelled when the Hardy boys find a real Spanish doubloon. From that point on, the plot thickens from one episode to another, complete with convicts and police. In the final ominous and scary episode, the Hardy boys discover the long-lost treasure and emerge as heroes, proving their ability as top-notch detectives.

"There was a very spooky element about that serial," said Tommy Kirk, who was just fourteen years old at the time. "There was an old house and a lot of suspense and dark doings. I mean, it wasn't exactly *Friday the 13th* but in its own way it was pretty creepy."

Auditioning for the role of Joe Hardy was not Kirk's first tryout at the Disney Studio. "About a year earlier I auditioned for 'Spin and Marty' but didn't get it, although I never got a chance to read for any part. It was an open audition and the casting people just had us play baseball out on the grass and observed us. Actually, I never even got to bat!" For "The Hardy Boys," auditions were a bit different. Kirk was given a long passage to perform with 15-year-old Tim Considine. "I remember that we were supposed to be hot on the trail of a crook in the scene," said Kirk. "A few weeks later, I found out that I got the role."

Kirk came to his acting job at Disney having appeared onstage at the Pasadena Playhouse in a revival of Eugene O'Neill's *Ah, Wilderness!* But it was his role on "The Hardy Boys" that launched a

Tim Considine (left) and Tommy Kirk (right) were junior-detective brothers on "The Hardy Boys" serial.

successful Disney career, which kept him under contract to the studio from 1956 to 1963. After completing a second "Hardy Boys" serial entitled "The Mystery of Ghost Farm," Kirk went on to star in a variety of Disney feature films, including *Old Yeller*, *The Shaggy Dog* (along with Tim Considine and Kevin Corcoran), *Swiss Family Robinson*, and *The Absent-Minded Professor*.

Although he spent two years as part of "The Mickey Mouse Club," he never really became good friends with any of the Mouseketeers. "We weren't close friends because we lived in two different worlds," Kirk explained. "I was not a Mouseketeer at any stage of the game, I was just in the series. But I knew all the kids, — you know to say 'hi' in the commissary — and I'd sometimes see them in the trailer schoolhouse. But I don't remember going to any parties or anything that they went to. It's funny, because we worked on two soundstages literally next door to each other."

The serials contributed greatly to the success of "The Mickey Mouse Club" and in 1956, the show, with all its popular elements, was revolutionizing children's television. It was in that year that "The Mickey Mouse Club" hit the peak of its success.

8

THE SECOND SEASON

As all teenagers, we went through the same growing process
as the kid next door. We had natural crushes on each other,
but after a while, the crushes turned into friendships.

— Mouseketeer TOMMY COLE

"TOMMY COLE AND I WENT STEADY for a couple of weeks," said Sharon Baird. "Going steady" for young teenagers on the Disney lot reflected a quaint and endearing simplicity. "There was a vending machine at the studio with all different kinds of candy and Tommy knew Butter Brickle was my favorite. So when I wasn't in the classroom he'd put a Butter Brickle bar in my desk for me to find when I got back."

Tommy Kirk also spent a brief time "going with" Sharon. "We became blood brother and sister," she explained. "We pricked our index fingers so they would bleed, and then held them together. I think our blood kinship lasted about two weeks." The youngsters

The
second-season
contingent
of Mouseketeers.

showed their affection in innocent ways, and as Sharon added, "We never really went out on a date. Just working together all the time you sort of became like brother and sister. The crushes would fade."

"Darlene was also a heartthrob of mine," said Tommy Cole. "It was a love-hate relationship in that we were very jealous of each other. I think because we were the only singers in the core group on the show it caused friction between us. But our infatuations with each other blew over quickly and we just became friends."

"Karen and Cubby were the babies," added Doreen. "Poor little Karen, she just used to follow the herd. We dragged her everywhere and we'd always say, 'Karen, are you okay?' and she'd look up at us as if to say, 'Yeah, I'm okay, I'm not a baby you know!'"

"Karen and I became friends even though she was younger," said Sharon. "I would help her with dancing and stuff. We called each other special names; one of us was 'Peaches' and the other was 'Puddin'.' Cubby, however, being the youngest along with Karen, was her closest compatriot on the show." "Cubby and I not only did everything together but we argued a lot," explained Karen. "If Cubby said it was green, I would say it was blue. We disagreed on everything, but we were together all the time. We even used to play canasta together during lunchtime. We took dancing lessons together, horseback riding lessons together and swimming lessons together. Everyone thought we'd grow up and get married."

Karen and Cubby were paired together onstage and off.

Cubby, who acquired that nickname because his mother thought he looked like a little bear cub when he was born, had an unmistakable twinkle of mischief in his blue eyes. "Karen and I were a team. Being the two youngest kids, they liked to put us together," Cubby remarked. "We sang duets together, did feature segments together, and usually got in trouble together."

"My first real buddy-buddy was Darlene," recalled Doreen Tracey. "She was brilliant and so funny. We used to play so well off each other. I also liked Annette, because she was calm, a soothing force for me." During the second year of the show, friendships matured and "we started going off in groups," explained Doreen. "I hung out with Annette and Cheryl Holdridge. Sharon was friends with everybody. She was kind of everyone's buddy." Annette and Sharon also became best of friends.

"My closest friend of all the Mouseketeers was and still is Sharon," said Annette.

Roy Williams and Jimmie Dodd help Karen celebrate her birthday.

The two teenagers gravitated toward each other because "we kind of had the same temperament," said Sharon. "We both have a shy side to us and she was down-to-earth no matter how popular she became. She remained sweet and never changed and I was attracted to that quality."

"The Mickey Mouse Club" friendships also extended beyond the children to the adult members of the club. Jimmie Dodd and Roy Williams looked over their flock on and off the soundstage. "I remember when I was nine, Roy let me have a birthday party at his house," Karen said. "It was a swimming party, and I think there were more people there than

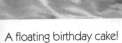

A floating birthday cake!

Lots of fun for the Mouseketeers at Karen's birthday pool party at Roy's house.

Jimmie and Darlene party in song.

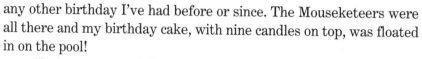

any other birthday I've had before or since. The Mouseketeers were all there and my birthday cake, with nine candles on top, was floated in on the pool!

"I always thought Roy was very jolly," Karen added. "He was very, very sweet to me." "He was a real friend of mine, too," added Annette. "Roy was the clown and he really kept everybody up in spirit. He was always drawing caricatures of people. I mean, every time you made a move he had a picture for you and he'd rip it off the easel and give it to you. I've kept a lot of those pictures in my scrapbook."

Director Sid Miller remembered the sketches as well. "Roy was always drawing things of everybody. If I was talking about something, he would immediately draw it to fit the conversation. And he was always on the set with a pad and pencil whether he was in a shot or not. He had a big smile

Roy passes out the hot dogs to hungry Mouseketeers.

Doreen and Roy share a fun moment on the set.

and was so proud to be on the show. He couldn't wait to sing that song, 'M-I-C-K-E-Y.'"

Of Jimmie Dodd, Karen recalled, "Jimmie was very religious; a really good person. He and his wife, Ruth, were just wonderful all the time. I always remember him holding us together. Jimmie was our leader, he truly was."

Tommy's memories of Big Mooseketeer Roy were a bit different from those that nine-year-old Karen recalled. "Roy was our token dirty old man," said Tommy, with a smile.

Roy doing what he did best.

Jimmie and Ruth Dodd share a relaxing time in their backyard.

Roy and Jimmie at work off the set.

117

"He was wonderful, likable, and he loved all of us. But he always made little off-color jokes or remarks, which, of course, we as kids loved. I think if Mr. Disney knew about some of the things he was telling us, he wouldn't have been too happy. Jimmie, on the other hand, was just the opposite. There was absolutely nothing risqué about him. He would never tell an off-color joke. If he did, we sure didn't hear it. Jimmie was sort of a father figure, like Walt Disney."

Walt Disney requested that the kids call him "Uncle Walt," although "Mr. Disney" seemed to be the salutation most often used. "I could never call him 'Uncle Walt,'" remarked Annette. "I respected him so much, I just couldn't be that familiar." "I had great respect for

him too," said Tommy. "I didn't realize at the time that the buck stopped with him. I knew he was Walt Disney, a very famous man, and we were working at his studio. But I really didn't grasp what that meant."

Walt Disney entertains with card tricks during a break on "The Mickey Mouse Club" set.

Walt Disney surrounded by a group of Mouseketeers, also including "Spin and Marty's" Tim Considine and David Stollery, Tommy Kirk, and Kevin "Moochie" Corcoran.

Despite his high regard for the big boss, Tommy does have the unique distinction of asking Walt Disney to leave the set. "I was doing a scene one day and having a hard time with the cue cards when Walt Disney came in. I was so nervous with him there I just couldn't get it right and had to ask him to leave. Fortunately, he understood and, in fact, made the comment 'I'd better get out of here!' Once he left, I was fine."

"I always thought of Walt Disney as a shy man," said Sharon. "I could tell he was always watching out for us, and I remember him in coveralls with paint all over like any one of many workers on the lot. And he knew everyone on a first-name basis, whether it was a producer or director or a gardener or electrician. Of course, he knew all the Mouseketeers by name. But," she said laughing, "he had an advantage with us — we had our names in big black letters across our chest!"

"He didn't talk down, at least not to me," said Doreen, of her memories of Walt Disney. "I'll never forget doing a scene with him for a Donald Duck television special at Disneyland. In between the shooting, he turned to me and said, 'Do you realize that this is the greatest thing you will ever do in your whole life?' At first, I thought, What does he mean by that? But I never forgot it and boy, was he ever right."

Walt Disney's bigger-than-life image sometimes intimidated. "I was frightened of him," said Virginia Funicello. "I actually hid when I saw him coming. But he was really so nice and he knew I was scared. To me, he was such a big man and I was just a stupid housewife, and didn't know anything about show business. He always tried to make me feel comfortable, though, by talking about Annette and telling me what a wonderful girl he thought she was."

Sid Miller (left), Walt Disney (center), and Bill Walsh (right) confer on the set.

Annette also felt especially close to him. "He was so supportive of me," she recalled. "I certainly wasn't the best singer and wasn't the best dancer on the show, but he always made me feel better about myself."

Although idolized as they were across the nation on television, most of the Mouseketeers' home life was surprisingly ordinary. "I had my chores to do at home just like any other kid," said Sharon. "Sometimes the neighbor kids would wait for me to come home at night to find out what I had done that day, and they'd ask about Annette or Bobby, but mostly my life at home was pretty normal."

Doreen catches up on some fan mail.

Annette whips up Sunday morning breakfast.

Tommy Cole enjoys a lazy day at home.

"I was living in Long Beach," explained Bobby. "My folks didn't ever think they should move to Hollywood, U.S.A. I have an older brother and two sisters and my parents had to think of them too. Besides, they wanted to keep my feet on the ground." Tommy's parents agreed with that philosophy as well. "My mom and dad were non-pros," said Tommy. "My dad was a salesman and mom was a housewife. I was in show business because I wanted to do it, although my mother clearly told me that if I ever let it go to my head I would be out of the business."

While many of the kids on the show were growing together as a family, by the end of shooting the second-year series there was one member of the adult crew, Bob Amsberry, who was let go for reasons never clearly stated. When told of the dismissal, Amsberry was shattered and wrote a letter to Walt Disney detailing his feelings.

"I had hoped my work on 'The Mickey Mouse Club' would be the beginning of a long and lasting career at the Walt Disney Studio and the climax of a dream that began when I was nine years old," Amsberry wrote. "I would like to stay on here in hope I could someday produce, direct, or be placed in a supervisory position. I am willing to learn, and above all willing to work, and if necessary at a reduced salary." (Amsberry was earning $160 per week at the time.)

What Amsberry did not know was that his dismissal was long overdue. Walt Disney had wanted him dropped from the payroll after the first season of the show and had written a memo to Bill Anderson in early 1956 regarding the matter. "I wish you would check on the status of Bob Amsberry," Disney stated in his memo. "I feel he is still on our payroll, but I do not know why. Also check on everybody in the Mouseketeer group who has been carried over. I believe that outside of the nine Mouseketeers, Jimmie Dodd and Roy Williams, we should

Annette, Sharon, and Cheryl knit during an onstage break.

start from scratch." Ever cost conscious, Walt continued, "Let's make a thorough check on the setup of the Mouseketeers and see that we are not carrying people who are not needed."

Amsberry left the studio in September 1956 in the hope of continuing his entertainment career. Tragically, just over a year later, on November 21, 1957, he was killed in an automobile accident. Amsberry was just twenty-nine years old.

The Mouseketeers themselves became victims of a ghoulish series of rumors that spread throughout the country in mid-'56. The Cleveland *News* reported: "Who keeps spreading rumors from coast to coast that Walt Disney's Mouseketeers have been killed or injured in some accident and why? And it's been going on for many months. Despite prompt denials, the rumbles spread. Fans deluged the studio with letters asking whether the reports were true. TV stations got up to two hundred telephone calls daily. About 5 percent of the letters report death and injury rumors and ask whether they're true. Here's a sampling — a boy, ten, from Danville, Virginia: *'Some children at choir practice today told me that some of the Mouseketeers had been killed in a bus wreck.'*"

A girl from Woodland Hills, California: "*There have been rumors going around that Annette and Darlene are dead and Cubby has a broken leg which happened on a roller coaster. We hope this rumor isn't true.*"

From Ada, Oklahoma: "*The sixth grade of Latta School would like to know if it is true that Annette and Karen were killed in a car accident and if Cubby was hurt. We sincerely hope it isn't true.*"

A girl in Rhode Island: "*I have heard a rumor that Annette was killed in a bus accident and that three of the boys were hurt...please set me straight.*"

To help squelch the insistent rumors, the Disney Studio issued a national press release: "Mouseketeers Alive and Squeaking." It stated, "False rumors that several of Walt Disney's Mouseketeers and adult Mouseketeer, Jimmie Dodd, have been killed or injured in an automobile accident again cropped up in the East. There is no truth to the reports.

"Most recent came from Hartford, Connecticut. Similar rumors originated in Massachusetts and spread rapidly among school children. In both instances, there was no foundation at all for the stories. One version of the first rumor, later corrected by the press, stated that Mouseketeer Annette Funicello was killed and Dodd was among the injured.

"The Mouseketeers currently are engaged in pre-production rehearsals at the Disney Studio in Burbank, California, for filming their 'Mickey Mouse Club' segments for the Fall season beginning October 1 over the ABC-TV Network."

A Disney spokesman further stated to the media, "I haven't the slightest idea what causes the rumors. Sure, there have been death rumors over the years about other people in Hollywood — Shirley Temple, Bing Crosby, Harold Lloyd and others, but they never lasted more than twenty-four hours. There's never been anything as sustained as this."

To set worried fans straight, the Disney Studio responded by sending them postcard-sized pictures of the Mouseketeers, with a printed message on the back assuring that they were all in good health. The rumors finally subsided.

The 1956 season group of seventeen Mouseketeers were indeed well and kicking, singing and dancing daily in their specialized segments for each of the Monday–Friday days of the week. Monday's "Fun with Music Day" was a favorite for several of the kids. The show opened with Mickey Mouse garbed as a song-and-dance man. The Mouseketeers, wearing their name shirt costume, sang and tap-danced to the first day of the week's song, — words and lyrics written by director Sidney Miller and Tom Adair:

It's time for fun with music,
Fun with music,
Making music is fun.
Whether it's a song of home or some foreign land,
Music is the language we all understand.
We're all for one with music,
Fun with music,
And before we are done
Just wait and see,
You'll all agree
Fun with music is fun,
Fun for everyone.

"I loved doing the songs and dances," said Sharon. "I remember doing the 'Edelweiss Polka' and the 'Sweet Shoppe Rock,' and we got to dress up in so many different costumes. The production numbers were definitely my favorite part."

"I loved doing specialty musical numbers," said Doreen, "where all the boys had to dance with me. Yeah, yeah, I liked that."

Tommy, not particularly noted for his dancing ability, had to work a little harder than the rest. "I had to try to stay up with them, and luckily Bobby, Sharon, and a few of the other kids really helped me an awful lot. Fortunately, the choreographer was smart enough not to give me anything that was real difficult."

Doreen and Bobby trip the light fantastic.

On Tuesday's "Guest Star Day" show, Mickey opened the festivities in formal white tie and tails attire and asked the unseen audience, "Everybody neat and pretty?" "Neat and pretty!" came the affirmative reply. The Mouseketeers, boys in jackets and bow ties and girls in pinafore-type dresses, sang and danced to the opening number while moving in and out of full-size door facades, each featuring Mickey and the Mouseketeer's name on the outside. The tune "Today Is Tuesday" featured music and lyrics by Jimmie Dodd:

Annette, Jimmie, and Bobby introduce "Guest Star Day."

Today is Tuesday, you know what that means,
We're gonna have a special guest
So get out the broom
And sweep the place clean
And dust off the mat
So the welcome can be seen.
Roll out the carpet,
Strike up the band,
And give out with a "Hip, Hooray!" ("Hip, Hooray!")
Wiggle your ears
Like good Mouseketeers —
We're gonna present a guest today
'Cause Tuesday is "Guest Star Day!"

Among the many guest stars who appeared on "The Mickey Mouse Club" Tuesday segment were the singing Lennon Sisters; comedy stars Judy Canova, Morey Amsterdam, and Jerry Colonna; Clarence Nash, the voice of Donald Duck; Cliff Edwards, the voice of Jiminy Cricket; and Fess Parker and Buddy Ebsen, as well as a huge roster of other talented performers.

Roy Williams with actress/comedienne Judy Canova.

The Lennon Sisters.

Morey Amsterdam entertains the kids.

There were a few very famous personalities who were approached about appearing on the show but never quite made it. Mickey Rooney turned down the appearance over salary. Interoffice "Mickey Mouse Club" correspondence indicated: "Regarding the possibility of Mickey Rooney doing a Guest Star spot on the show, this is

Cliff Edwards, the voice of Jiminy Cricket, guests on the show.

Buddy Ebsen and Fess Parker, the stars of Disney's "Davy Crockett" trilogy, visit "The Mickey Mouse Club."

to advise that in speaking with his manager, I was advised that the salary offered is completely out of the question. When he mentioned a salary from $5,000 to $10,000 to do our show, I thanked him kindly and told him this was way beyond our budget."

Another famous guest who was invited to do the show was comedian Red Skelton. He wanted very much to do it and to feature his two children, Richard and Valentina, with him. But there were problems beyond his control. First, he had just signed a contract with CBS-TV to do his own show, and was contractually barred from making appearances on other networks or for other sponsors. However, Skelton wanted to do "The Mickey Mouse Club" so badly that he personally contacted CBS and insisted that they give him permission, which they did.

But there was yet a second hurdle to be scaled, and that had to do with sponsors. It seems one of the sponsors on Skelton's new show was the Pet Milk Company, and they would not permit him to appear on any other show where there was a conflicting sponsor involved, which, in the case of "The Mickey Mouse Club," was the Carnation Company. The end result — no appearance.

Wednesday's festivities heralded "Anything Can Happen Day" as Mickey flew onto the scene on a magic carpet wearing his sorcerer's robe and hat. The midweek melody had music and lyrics penned by Jimmie Dodd:

> Today is a day that is filled with surprises,
> Nobody knows what's gonna happen.
> Why, you might find yourself on an elephant on the moon
> Or riding in an auto underneath a blue lagoon.
> Yes, we Mouseketeers think you're gonna have some thrills,
> And you know it's true that a laugh can cure your ills.
> And so, if you're pleasure bent,
> We are glad to present
> The Mouseketeers' "Anything Can Happen Day."

The Mouseketeers appeared in this fun segment in a vast array of costumes, among them: Cubby, a bunny wearing a top hat; Karen, a ballerina puppet in a tutu, her strings guided by Big Mooseketeer Roy in Bavarian guise; Annette, decked out as a flapper; Tommy, a fireman; Cheryl, a bird in a gilded cage; Darlene, a seaside beauty of the 1920s; Lonnie, a cowboy; Jimmie, an astronaut; Sharon, an Indian

"Anything Can Happen Day"

girl; and Bobby, tailored in formal wear, riding across the set on a unicycle, an ability he had to acquire for the number.

"There was some competition among the kids on the show," Bobby recalled. "If you were asked if you knew how to do a particular thing, you always said yes. And then you learned. When they asked me if I could ride a unicycle, 'Of course,' I said, and then had to get a guy from the circus to teach me how in my backyard at home. The thing was, you wanted to get in front of that camera as much as possible."

"Circus Day," on Thursday, showcased bandleader Mickey while the Mouseketeers were elaborately attired in circus costumes that ranged from clown to weight lifter to a bearded lady. Jimmie Dodd, once again, was responsible for words and lyrics to Thursday's song:

Here comes the circus,
Everyone loves the circus
And that includes the Merry Mouseketeers.
Clowns in the circus
Keep the frowns from the circus
As the old calliope rings in your ears (boop, boop).
There'll be lions, tigers, elephants,
And lots of things inside,
And there's a man who's nine feet tall
And a lady five feet wide.
And so, hooray for the circus!
Now, away for the circus,
You're the guests of the Merry Mouseketeers!

Many world-class circus acts appeared on "The Mickey Mouse Club," showcasing, among others, their talents as acrobats, trampolinists, magicians, tumblers, and clowns. A variety of animal acts, with names like Captain Winston and His Seals, Pansy the Horse, and Gentry's Chimps, featured dogs, cats, seals, horses, elephants, monkeys, lions, and bears.

The "Mickey Mouse Club" week ended on Friday with "Talent Round-Up Day." Mickey closed out the week-long fun on a western theme, wearing a ten-gallon hat and spinning a lariat. He launched the show with a friendly "Hi, pardners!" to ready us to join the Mouseketeers clothed in their best cowboy and cowgirl finery. Music for Friday's song was written by George Bruns, lyrics by Gil George (pseudonym for frequent contributing lyricist, studio nurse Hazel George):

Saddle your pony, here we go
Down to the talent rodeo.
Gather up Susie, Jack and Joe,
Join the talent round-up.
Round 'em up, bring 'em in,
Everybody's sure to win.
Step right up, here we go,
Oh, what a rodeo!
Bring along Dinah, Bob and Bill,
Ask everybody on the hill.
We're gonna have a great big thrill,
Join the talent round-up.
Round 'em up, bring 'em in,
Everybody's sure to win.
Step right up, here we go,
Oh, what a rodeo!
Bring along Mary, Jim and Moe,
Ask everybody you may know.
We're gonna have a great big show,
Join the talent round-up.
Step right up, step right up,
Here we go, here we go,
Join the round-up rodeo!

It was this segment of "The Mickey Mouse Club" that featured many of the children who won appearances on the show through the National Talent Round-Up promotions held throughout the country. During the segment, guests performed while the Mouseketeers looked on. At the end of their act, and after much Mouseketeer applause, the guest was made an Honorary Mouseketeer by the Mouse Club troupe themselves, and presented with a scroll, gilded mouse ears, and cowboy hat to the jingle:

"You're an Honorary Mouseketeer."

Step right up
(Step right up),
Here's your hat
(Here's your hat),
What a hat
(What a hat),
Here's your ears…
Reach right out,
Time is here.
You're an honorary
Mouseketeer!

While children sang, danced, and laughed through each day of the week with the Mouseketeers, other segments of "The Mickey Mouse Club" were clearly geared to a kind of fun different from the whimsical sort we enjoyed with the Mouseketeers. They were designed to educate with fun, long before "Sesame Street" was even a twinkle in anyone's eye.

9
EDUCATION
IN DISGUISE

It's the encyclopedia, E-N-C-Y-C-L-O-P-E-D-I-A.
Just look inside this book and you will see, everything
from "A" clear down to "Z."

— JIMINY CRICKET

DIDN'T EVERYONE WHO WATCHED 'The Mickey Mouse Club' learn to spell encyclopedia this way?" Leonard Maltin has said. "That's still the way I spell it to this very day, with that same melodious cadence in my head." Viewers were instructed on the use of this magical book, which could unlock the mysteries of the world, by Jiminy Cricket, an appealing character who was cocky and streetwise and had gained fame as Pinocchio's faithful conscience in the 1940 classic Disney animated film.

Attired in a smart suit and top hat, Jiminy was filled with homespun wisdom, which he imparted to the viewing audience in the most entertaining ways. Cliff Edwards, a radio singer from Missouri known also as "Ukulele Ike," was the voice of the diminutive green insect, who had taught movie audiences that when you wish upon a star your dreams come true. Jiminy now had a new platform, television, to instill knowledge in the minds of millions of kids. He did so through several "Mickey Mouse Club" series: the "Encyclopedia" series; the "I'm No Fool" series; the "Mickey Mouse Book Club" series; the "Nature of Things"; and the "You" series.

From each of these, youngsters across the country learned many valuable lessons. One such learning session from the "Encyclopedia" series taught, in animation and live action footage, about milk. Opening to the "M" volume of the reference book, Jiminy, flipping the pages, says, "...Mackerel, microphone, milk, mineral, Monterey...milk! Ya know, when I think of milk [as the bottle of milk on the page animates into a cow]...I think of good ole Bossy the dairy cow, one of nature's marvels, turning grass and grain into milk. She's a regular factory!"

Jiminy continued while photos and film clips illustrated his story: "Columbus brought the first cattle to America in 1493. And in the year 1611, the first dairy cow appeared in the Jamestown colony — oh — that was in Virginia! Today, some of the most popular dairy cows are the Holstein, which came from Holland in 1795, the Jersey from the Isle of Jersey in 1815...eh, that's one of the Channel Islands between England and France...the Ayrshire from Scotland in 1822, and the Guernsey from the Isle of Guernsey in 1831. Hmm. That's right next to the Isle of Jersey!

"Now, listen to this! There are over twenty-four million dairy cows in this country. With all that milk, we should really be healthy! Y'know, at milking time [Jiminy turns on a radio — gets hot music]...dairy cows like music [Jiminy turns the radio dial to sweet music]...the uh, right kind, of course.

"Milking is done twice a day with modern sterilized machines. Once the milk leaves the cow, it is cooled and sent to a receiving station where it is checked for freshness. Then it is weighed. Weighed!? What d'ya know? Milk is measured in pounds instead of quarts because the more butter fat it has, the more it weighs. And it's richer too.

"At the bottling plant, many tests are made. Boy, are they careful! And speaking of being careful…in the late 1800s Louis Pasteur, a Frenchman, made a great discovery. He found a method of killing bacteria — germs, that is — in milk. That's what this machine is for. It's called a pasteurizer. It heats milk to a hundred and forty-five degrees for thirty seconds, then quickly cools it off. Some pasteurized milk is homogenized in this machine. Milk and cream are mixed so well they never separate. Homogenized milk has the same consistency throughout. This homogenizing is done under two thousand pounds of pressure. Hmm! Mashed milk!"

Jiminy completed the lesson, "The final step is bottling. Boy, look at those caps go on! Yes sir, milk is good to drink and it's made into cheese and butter and ice cream and…oh, lots of things. And who do we have to thank for all this? Bossy here. Y'know, with all his knowledge man has never been able to make a machine to replace the cow."

Among the myriad topics that were included in Jiminy's assorted lesson plans were: "You and Your Five Senses," "The Human Animal," "The Living Machine," "The Camel," "The Elephant," and "The Horse"; from the "I'm No Fool" series — "I'm No Fool as a Pedestrian," "I'm No Fool Having Fun," "I'm No Fool on a Bicycle," "…with Fire," "…in Water." Children were taught about America's railroads, Navajo jewelry, and steel, among many other things.

Jiminy also introduced the Newsreel Specials on the show with the "Encyclopedia" opening, turning to the topic in the book that would be presented that day on the Special. The episodes, which were usually narrated by one of the Mouseketeers as a Mouseketeer

"I'm No Fool as a Pedestrian" was a Jiminy Cricket lesson.

reporter, were filmed on location and featured youngsters on the scene actually taking part in the story.

"Inside Report on Washington — the FBI," a four-part newsreel series, took us behind the scenes of the FBI. The inside story of the world-famous organization opened at the Marine Corps base at Quantico, Virginia, the home of the FBI Academy where new agents are trained. The story proceeds to the FBI Identification Bureau where Dirk Metzger, the young on-scene reporter, challenges the head of the Division to identify him by his fingerprints alone. (He had been fingerprinted once before, when he qualified for a fingerprint merit badge in the Boy Scouts.) After he is fingerprinted once again in order to begin the search, the process of matching the prints to his identity unfolds.

The narrator of the story — in this case, Mouseketeer Tommy Cole — explained that there are 146,000,000 (in 1957) fingerprints on file, all classified by arches, loops, whirls, etc. As he further explained, "A name means nothing — names can change, but fingerprints never." Through a filing process (no doubt computerized today), Dirk's "on file" fingerprints were matched with his new prints within minutes. The millions of kids watching witnessed the actual process, through the eyes of a contemporary, and in language and visuals they could well understand. It was fascinating.

They were also treated to reports on Congress, how U.S. coins are minted, the White House, how news is gathered, how Japanese geishas are trained. Viewers visited the *Nautilus*, were taken aboard a whaling ship, climbed the Alps with a group of American youngsters, explored the atom, and were tutored on the American two-party system — with a special message from Walt Disney:

Hi Mouseketeers! Next Tuesday will be Election Day. Now I know that most of you enjoying our "Mickey Mouse Club" shows are not old enough to vote. But there is one thing every one of you can do right now for the good of our country. Each one of you can remind your mothers and fathers, respectfully, that a full vote on Tuesday means a true majority will select the Government we will have for the next four years.

Now it doesn't matter to which party your family belongs. What does matter is that every grownup in your family votes. Just remember: your job is to remind mother and dad, with all respect that good

Mouseketeers show to their parents, that Tuesday is Election Day — the day to vote!

In addition to the multi-part Newsreel Specials, "Mickey Mouse Club" newsreels, featured three times a week, also kept children involved, informed and aware of the world around them. These were the first series of television newsreel features produced specifically for young people. Film material for the newsreels was gathered from some fifty veteran cameramen on location in the United States in such cities as Seattle, San Francisco, Denver, Tucson, Chicago, Detroit, Louisville, New Orleans, Houston, New York, and Philadelphia, as well as in cities of many foreign countries. Globally, photographic units were stationed in Scandinavia, France, Germany, Turkey, Spain, Greece, Kenya, India, Italy, Austria, Cuba, Mexico, Peru, Chile, Argentina, and Brazil, including Rio de Janeiro, São Paulo, and the Amazon River community of Manaus. Entertainment, combined with information, was emphasized in each edition, which contained between four and six stories or news features.

Walt Disney believed that young people were interested in what others of their generation were doing, wherever they were growing up. In keeping with that focus, the newsreel features covered youth at work, at play, engaging in hobbies and in sports, individually and in groups. Reported in the old-fashioned movie house "Movietone News"-style, stories focused on topics that were interesting and informative to youngsters, whether it was a story on "Who Named the Teddy Bear?" or "There's Money in Honey" — or "The Littlest Golfer," about a five-year-old with a remarkable knack for the game.

"I thought the newsreel segment was real interesting," said Bobby Burgess. "Instead of making the show just about kids having fun, they thought about showing the viewing audience what other kids were doing all around the world. I remember in school we always had our *Weekly Reader*s to read about those things, but to see them happening right in front of our eyes was great."

"It wasn't just cartoons and Mouseketeers," recalled Mouseketeer Lonnie Burr. "Kids were taught how Christmas was celebrated in other lands and how life was lived on a farm. They learned something while they were being entertained."

Educators around the country enthusiastically endorsed "The Mickey Mouse Club," and the Hollywood trade paper, *Variety*, reported that the show represented "Walt Disney's genius for wholesome and skillful integration of educational and entertainment values."

Walt Disney and the ABC Television Network further underscored their commitment to education (and promotion of their shows) by distributing their *Disney on Television Class-*

Mouseketeer Tommy Cole (left) and reporter Dirk Metzger (right) took viewers "Inside the FBI."

room Guide to teachers throughout the country. Within the booklet were synopses of individual programs, advance schedules giving program dates and times, program notes, and guide sheets suggesting classroom activities, and other appropriate items.

With regard to "The Mickey Mouse Club," Walt Disney stated in the 1955 edition of the *Guide:* "It is our belief the subject matter for such a program need not necessarily be restricted to the kinds of things which are traditionally offered on 'children's programs.' We feel the interests of young people are very broad, and we hope to challenge as many of these interests as possible. Portions of 'The Mickey Mouse Club' will touch on travel, science, health, vocational planning, sports, literature and many other things. We have the greatest respect for the basic intelligence of our future adults and their desire to learn. We, likewise, are aware of a sometimes prevalent habit of 'talking down' to audiences of this type. To the best of our ability we aim to 'talk up' as much as possible as we program our material, remembering that we will accomplish more if we 'entertain' as we go along."

The "What I Want to Be" series featured a young boy and girl who were given the rare opportunity to experience every phase in the operation of a modern airline, while the kids at home were given food for thought about future careers. "Foreign Correspondent" took viewers on tours of historic sites in cities abroad, and Sooty the puppet, the number one television star in England, brought an international flavor of fun into our living rooms.

The members of the baby boom generation who tuned in to "The Mickey Mouse Club" every day were fortunate to be exposed to children's television at this level. It wasn't until more than a decade later, in the late '60s, that Joan Ganz Cooney, founder and president of the Children's Television Workshop, would create a revolutionary new program called "Sesame Street," which would entertain as well as educate. Could it be that its roots were nurtured in a black-and-white series starring Mickey Mouse? Of the many costumed characters of "Sesame Street," Oscar the Grouch is the most popular. Scruffy, green, and cantankerous, he inhabits a New York City trash can. His protégés, four-year-olds wearing green T-shirts and trashcan lids tied under their chins, are called Grouseketeers.

The current new-age star of the preschool generation is Barney, a pudgy, fuzzy, non-aggressive *Tyrannosaurus rex* who stars on his own television show, called, "Barney & Friends." Unlike "Sesame Street," which focuses on educational fundamentals with eclectic visuals, Barney's success is based more on its relaxed pace and emphasis on emotional concerns. "When I interviewed the ladies who created Barney, right at the beginning before it really caught on," explained Leonard Maltin, "they told me then that one of the things they remembered was how strongly they related to the kids on 'The Mickey Mouse

The "What I Want to Be" series took viewers aboard a modern jetliner.

Club' in their own childhoods. From that memory they felt it very important to use kids on their show that children at home could relate to. So the principle still held and worked for them, because it's not just the dinosaur that made that series successful, it is the kids surrounding it. Kids relate to kids." Indeed, in a magazine interview, Kathy Parker, one of three producers of "Barney & Friends," recalled a happy, stable childhood, but admitted, "The only time I would cry was if I had to miss the Mouseketeers."

Along with the variety of educational segments on "The Mickey Mouse Club" were daily interludes near the end of each show devoted to a delightful instruction known as the Doddism, dedicated to principles for good living. Jimmie Dodd, the genial host, friend, and father figure for kids on and off the show, usually delivered the adage or assigned it to one of the Mouseketeers. Doddisms covered a multitude of how-to-live-happily subjects encompassing, among others, philosophy, education, beauty, and laughter.

Strumming his Mousegetar, a one-of-a-kind, four-string tenor guitar that incorporated Mickey Mouse's face onto the front of the instrument, Jimmie Dodd imparted his words of wisdom in a kindhearted, sincere, and soothing manner that was utterly magnetic. For example, he taught kids about proverbs: "Hi, Mouseketeers. Do you know what proverbs are? They're say-

Jimmie Dodd taught that "Proverbs help us all to be better Mouseketeers."

ings that tell us in a few words a whole lot of wisdom." Strumming the Mousegetar, he sang:

> Proverbs, proverbs, they're so true,
> Proverbs tell us what to do;
> Proverbs help us all to be
> Better Mouseketeers.

He continued, "Here's a proverb: 'A wise man thinks *twice* before he speaks *once*.' Now, this proverb tells us that we should think over carefully what we're going to say so that what we *do* say will be the right thing. Then we won't have to be sorry for having said it — and that's important — because a word spoken in haste, without thinking, might hurt someone and cannot be retracted. So, Mouseketeers, think twice before you say something — once for what you're going to say and once for how it's going to affect others. Then you'll never be sorry for what you have said."

"Words to Grow By" were also part of the Doddism repertoire and frequently featured Mouseketeers musically delivering the message of the day. Bobby Burgess sang:

> The race is won by running —
> There is no other way;
> And if you keep on running,
> You will win one day.
>
> Suppose you study music;
> There is no other way —
> You have to practice music;
> Then you will play one day.
>
> So dig right in and do it now —
> Whatever should be done;
> You're a dope to sit and mope
> When everything is fun!

Mouseketeers Doreen, Annette and Darlene each taught us in song:

Beauty is as beauty does —
That's what wise men say;
Now, if you would be beautiful,
Do this every day:
Listen to your teacher,
Because she is well trained;
This is what she has to say —
"A beauty needs a brain."

Knowledge and discovery were instilled in the collective consciousness of a generation within these brief moments on a simple black and white, small screen, non-eclectic, children's television program. It was through Jimmie Dodd and the Mouseketeers that these popular words of wisdom became a part of our culture, "He who has health has hope, and he who has hope, has everything," "Self-confidence is the sure knowledge of our abilities and something we should all cultivate," "Patience is one of the most important virtues one can have in life," and "You must learn to walk before you can run."

One of Jimmie's favorite Doddisms and one that summed up his personal philosophy, was from the French philosopher Etienne De Grolier: "I expect to pass through life but once. If therefore, there be any kindness I can show, or any good thing I can do, to any fellow being, let me do it now and not defer or neglect it, as I shall not pass this way again."

"Jimmie was great," said Leonard Maltin. "He just had a personality that was irresistible and fatherly in the best possible way. His Doddisms were always very gentle and positive and never accompanied by any kind of scolding posture or negativity. He had an earnestness and warmth for what he was doing. He had heart."

"He was one of the nicest human beings I've ever known in my life," said Sharon Baird. "He was genuine and he didn't speak down to kids, he included them. He was a great person to look up to."

Tommy Cole also recollected Jimmie fondly. "He was a great influence on me," he warmly explained. "I remember during the opening of Disneyland, I went up to him and touched his hair because it was this beautiful red color and no one ever saw it because we were on black and white television. Mostly though, what I remember about Jimmie was that he was always kind, and man enough to say, 'I'm sorry.'"

"He was a very religious fellow," Lonnie Burr remarked. "One thing I liked about him was that he did not impinge his religious views on anybody. He was a really nice guy, exactly the same offstage as on. No variance whatsoever. And the Doddisms were wonderful. They took a stance; a very soft stance, but a stance."

Doreen Tracey perhaps best summed up the overall feeling of the Mouseketeers of their experiences with Jimmie Dodd. "He always gave us the feeling that we could do it, whatever it was. If we said, 'Can we do this or can we do that?,' his response was always the same. With a big smile, he'd say, 'Sure you can!'" With the enormous popularity of the show in its second season, it certainly seemed that the Mouseketeers could indeed do it all.

Another entertainment plus on "The Mickey Mouse Club" was the daily cartoons, featured in the show's final Mousecartoon segment. Derived from an enormous treasure of Disney animated shorts that had delighted theatergoers for years, these cartoons were television's first to capture the attention of children. At that time, there were no Saturday morning action-adventure superheroes or green-eyed monsters and goblins to become engrossed in. It was merely Mickey Mouse, Donald Duck, Goofy, and the rest of the gang.

In addition to the fun-filled pen-and-ink doings of the various characters, the cartoons also traced the history of the Disney art of

Donald Duck about to be foiled, as he was every day, when he struck the Mickey Mouse Club gong.

animation from some of Walt's earliest efforts in the field. "Steamboat Willie," the first synchronized sound cartoon, was part of the collection, along with Disney's famous Silly Symphonies. Interestingly, through the popularity and vast viewing audience of "The Mickey Mouse Club," the Disney cartoons were seen *each day* by a larger audience than had seen them during their entire theatrical release.

In the 1956 season of the show, viewers were also treated

to a series called "Animal Biographies," as well as several serialized segments on "The American Indians, the First Americans." They were given a bird's-eye view of nature's wonders on a "Sierra Pack Trip" series, learned "The Secret of Mystery Lake," and took "A Mousekatour to Samoa."

Youngsters continued to learn with 10-year-old Mouseketeer Sherry Alberoni, on several segments of "Anything Can Hap-

Mickey Mouse in "Steamboat Willie."

"Meeska, Mooska, Mouseketeer; Mousecartoon time now is here!"

pen Day," when she showed us what it was like to be a firefighter in the filmed segment "Rookie Fireman." Sherry, along with a world-famous photographer, also took us to the San Diego zoo where viewers discovered how to use and have fun with a camera.

Into its second season, "The Mickey Mouse Club" had shattered the competition. According to a ratings analysis, in addition to delivering an audience of over 12,000,000 children, it also attracted a large adult audience — in fact, 44% more adults than the average *adult* weekday program. And "The Mickey Mouse Club" provided another extra dimension in the form of 3,114,000 *attentive listeners* — adults who *heard* but did not actively *watch* the show while they were performing household tasks. As a result, "The Mickey Mouse Club" delivered a total of almost 7,000,000 adults, of which 67% were women. The extra audience dimension was very attractive to S.O.S. Magic scouring pads and other "adult" products that were eventually added as show sponsors.

Everyone, it seemed, children and adults alike, was a fan of "The Mickey Mouse Club." They all had their favorite parts of the show and their favorite Mouseketeers. In the latter regard, Annette was far and away leading the pack.

10
ANNETTE

*There was no studio like the Disney Studio, nor a producer
like Walt Disney. You could sense his love for children
in his product.*

— ANNETTE FUNICELLO

FIFTEEN YEARS OLD AND THE IDOL of millions of "Mickey
Mouse Club" devotees, Annette was every young girl's best friend
and every young boy's dream girl. Following the debut of her own
"Annette" serial, she was receiving 6,000 fan letters a month, including a steady flow of gifts and marriage proposals. Fan mail was run-
ning in the following vein:

*My son is six years old and has shown no noticeable desire for
girls, but he insists on seeing you daily.*

*Annette, in my book, you are beautiful. I dream of you every
night.*

There are a lot of girls in my class, but I don't think of them. I think of you.

I'm not a very good looker, but I love you.

Her life was hectic and fun, and seemingly idealistic for the kids who watched the show every day. In a 1957 article in *Walt Disney's Magazine* (previously *Walt Disney's Mickey Mouse Club Magazine*), we had a chance to glimpse the private world of Annette:

The life of a Mouseketeer is a busy one, as Annette Funicello can tell you. She goes to school — a full-time job for most fifteen-year-olds. She works five hours a day on the set. At night she studies both her homework and the next day's script. On some weekends there are public appearances, often at Disneyland. Maybe once or twice a year there's a tour to the east coast or middle west or Texas.

But Annette wouldn't trade her job for anything. "I really like this kind of work. And I want to stay in show business. Someday," she says, with a faraway look in her brown eyes, "want to be a fine actress. Like Elizabeth Taylor. She's my favorite."

Annette works at a pace which would discourage most people — young or old. But one of her fellow actors once remarked, "She always finds time to have fun, no matter how busy her schedule." And her schedule is a tough one — no doubt about it. The Funicello family is closely knit, but Annette finds that only rarely can she share her time with her parents, and her two brothers, Joey, age 12, and Mike, six.

Annette's day starts early. When she has a 7 A.M. call at the Studio, she must get up at 5:30. Her mother drives her the five miles from their home to the Studio, where Annette attends school, even when not working before the cameras. Before going on the "The Mickey Mouse Club" soundstage, Annette checks in to "Uncle Dave" Newell, the makeup man who gets her ready for the TV cameras. In the ladies' wardrobe department, supervisor Gertie Casey checks to make sure Annette's Mouseketeer outfit is neatly pressed and fits just right and hairdresser Lois Murray gives the teenage Mouseketeer a final touch-up.

After work, it's home to dinner and studying her script and doing homework. Each night she writes in her diary before going to bed. She writes down her thoughts, her actions…and her wishes, too. Her bedroom furniture is pink (her favorite color), and the headboard over her bed has built-in shelves and bookcases. Annette's reading matter includes the *Girl Scout Handbook, Mother's Encyclopedia, Science Problems, On Stage Everyone!, Girl Scouts at Penguin Pass,* a Kay Tracy mystery, and a Nancy Drew mystery,

Annette relaxes at home with her family: (from left to right) brother Michael; mom, Virginia; and her brother Joey.

among others. It would seem that Annette has a crush on Guy Williams, who plays "Zorro." Two pictures of "Zorro" smile down at her from gold-painted frames over her bed.

Annette always goes to sleep with the radio playing. After she is sound asleep, her father tiptoes in and turns it off. Annette admits she would be lost without the radio. She turns it on first thing in the morning, and it plays all the time. Much as she enjoys listening to disc jockeys, she doesn't have much time for watching TV. She says, "By the time I get home, take off my makeup, study my script, and do my homework, it's time for bed. But I haven't missed 'Zorro' yet!"

Annette receives thousands of fan letters each week. Though some stars are given publicity buildups by their studios, this was not true with Annette. The producer of "The Mickey Mouse Club" TV show, Bill Walsh, stated, "During the first year we wanted all the Mouseketeers to get an equal chance. We wanted to let the viewers, the kids at home, decide who the future Mouseketeers should be." Since she first appeared on TV, there has been no doubt of her popularity — her fan mail total has equaled that of some of Hollywood's biggest stars.

Her hobbies are swimming, diving and horseback riding. Because she is swamped by admirers at public pools and Santa Monica beaches, she goes swimming at the homes of other Mouseketeers or friends. Quite clothes-conscious, her taste runs to striking sweater-Capri pants combinations. She almost always wears a contrasting silk scarf tied around her throat. She is also very much aware of clothing worn by her girl friends and by boys. For instance, she says she always notices a boy's socks. Sitting in the Disney Studio theater one day, she noted that David Stollery's socks did not match. "Do you know what that proves?" retorted David. "That proves I was tired when I got up this morning."

A daily visit to the wardrobe department.

With the popularity of her young daughter, Virginia Funicello remembered the sometimes hectic and unpredictable experiences of life with Annette. "There were so many things that happened," Virginia said. "Like that forty-city tour. We couldn't even wash our clothes because by morning

Last minute touch-up.

they wouldn't be dry. And she used to wear all those petticoats and they'd be all smashed by the time we got to the next town. Then I'd have to try to find an electric bulb backstage somewhere so that I could have some light to iron her clothes.

Photos of Guy Williams, Annette's heartthrob, who starred in "Zorro," encircle her mirror.

The stars of the "Annette" serial: Roberta Shore, Tim Considine, and Annette Funicello.

Then, I could never find a plug!"

"I don't think any of us were prepared for what happened with the show," Annette remarked. "It just took off like wildfire and it became the number one children's show in America. All of a sudden we had these people coming to our door wanting autographs. We had to change our phone number and couldn't eat dinner at night because someone was always at the door. And my little brother was selling my phone number! So, it changed our life-style but we just tried to keep everything in perspective as much as we could."

Annette's tremendous renown was also paying off in sales of Disney-licensed "Annette" merchandise. Successful sales of books, paper-doll cut-outs, coloring

Annette and Walt Disney, her mentor and friend.

books, jewelry, and other products were clear indication of the teenager's popularity. From her work in her own "Mickey Mouse Club" "Annette" serial, yet another, and long-term product was born, which ultimately led to the enhancement of her overall career. Annette records were about to make her an even bigger star.

"It was a great surprise that a serial was named after me," said Annette. "The first serial I worked on was one where I was called upon to live on a farm in Wisconsin. It was called 'Adventures in Dairyland' and it was a great experience. We actually lived right there on the farm and I learned how to milk cows and feed chickens. But the 'Annette' serial was something different than I had ever done before. I remember being fitted with a long hairpiece that came down to my waist and it was the first time I ever had long hair."

The serial relates the story of a teenage girl who has been raised simply but suddenly finds herself living with city relatives and obliged to cope with the more formal patterns of city life. Based on the book *Margaret*, by Janette Sebring Lowry, "Annette" shows the struggle of a small-town girl to gain poise and confidence in herself, even against jealousies, and her ultimate successful triumph over life's challenges. Co-starring in the series were Shelley Fabares, Roberta Shore, Tim Considine, David Stollery, and Annette's fellow Mouseketeers Sharon Baird, Cheryl Holdridge, Tommy Cole, and Doreen Tracey.

"The serial started my singing career quite by accident," said Annette. "I was doing the series playing a little country farm girl, and sang a song called 'How Will I Know My Love,' on a hayride. It was supposed to be humorous. After the show aired, I remember Walt Disney came to me one day and said, 'We've got to put this out on a single. We're getting fan letters like crazy, kids want to buy it.' And I said, 'I don't sing.' He said, 'Well, I'm signing you to a recording contract, young lady. You're singing.' I said, 'Yes sir,' and that's what started my singing career. It was so unexpected."

Annette, of all the Mouseketeers, maintained a close relationship with Walt Disney, who guided her throughout her career. "My first memory of Mr. Disney was absolutely being in awe of him because I was such a fan of his work," she said. "At first, I didn't even realize, deep down, what was technically going on in his mind until I actually got to know and talk with him and realized that everything stemmed from his great love of children and nature. Every time I saw him at Disneyland, he was always the engineer with the hat waving at everyone from the train. He was a kid at heart and I think his product shows that in everything he did.

"I remember him being on 'The Mickey Mouse Club' set all the time. Not that he picked us out separately and had conversations with us, but his presence was always felt." Annette really got to know Walt Disney after "The Mickey Mouse Club" ended; she was the only Mouseketeer to remain under studio contract. To Annette, Mr. Disney was the ideal boss who not only provided career support and guidance, but enriched her life in many personal ways.

"When I turned sixteen, Mr. Disney came to me with a script one day, and he knocked on the door of the little red trailer where I was going to school and said, 'Annette, I'd like to see you for a minute.' So I went outside and he presented me with a script and said, 'Happy Sweet Sixteen, you're appearing on 'Zorro.' I was so touched I started crying. He knew how I felt about Guy Williams. I mean, who could ask for a better boss?"

Sadly, Annette clearly remembers, too, the last time she saw Walt Disney. "I guess it was the latter part of 1965," she recalled (Disney died in 1966). "He was not feeling well, which not too many people knew about, and after I saw him, he wrote me a beautiful letter. In fact, over the course of my career he wrote me several letters which I've saved. But I haven't read them in many, many years," she said, filled with emotion. "I just can't."

Walt Disney did indeed orchestrate Annette Funicello's career, and perhaps the most intuitive judgment that he ever made for her was made in relation to her name. "When I was on 'The Mickey Mouse Club,' I went to Mr. Disney one day and told him that I wanted to change my last name because everyone mispronounced it," Annette explained. "I preferred Annette Turner to Annette Funicello. He looked at me and said, 'You have a beautiful Italian name, and once people learn how to pronounce it, they will never forget it.'" He was right.

Annette and the rest of the Mouseketeers were flying high. They were in demand and the public was clamoring to meet them. "My deepest wish is that the Mouseketeers would take a tour to every city, town, and state," wrote a devoted fan. The studio was eager to comply.

11
ON THE ROAD

Everywhere we went the reception was the same,
"simply fantastic." I've never seen such crowds
and enthusiasm.

— JIMMIE DODD

PUBLICITY, PUBLIC APPEARANCES, and promotional tours were part of the scenario to which the Mouseketeers were contractually bound. Therefore, when they were called upon to prepare for a particular photo shoot, department-store visit, or charity-event appearance, it was not presented as a request, but in writing as a matter-of-fact part of the job. A typical memo — in this case to Annette Funicello and Jimmie Dodd from Jack Lavin, one of the casting directors — stated:

"You are scheduled to make personal appearances as follows:

Friday, May 4th:	Broadway Valley Store at 6:45 p.m.
Saturday, May 5th:	Broadway downtown at 10:30 a.m.
	Broadway Crenshaw at 2 p.m.
	Broadway Hollywood at 4 p.m.

The Mouseketeers perform during a personal appearance.

"Your appearance will be in connection with autographing, etc., only — there will not be a show. You will be picked up at your respective homes — Annette and Mother, Friday 6 p.m., Saturday 9:30 a.m.; Jimmie Dodd, Friday, 6:20 p.m., Saturday 9:50 a.m.

"Pick up your Mouseketeers Costumes from the Wardrobe Department between 4 and 5 p.m. on Friday, May 4th. Please wear a

Riding in parades was part of the personal-appearance schedule.

At a charity dinner.

topcoat so that you will not easily be identifiable on the street. Thank you for your cooperation." (*Disney Studio instructions were brief and to the point.*)

Sometimes large Mouseketeer group appearances were scheduled for such things as charity benefits where the kids would actually perform in addition to signing autographs, being photographed, etc. While the Mouseketeer group was always handled with great care and treated well at such venues, parents and guardians accompanying them sometimes got the short end of the stick.

On one such occasion, at an event to raise funds for the Los Angeles John Tracy Clinic, the preparatory memo sent to the Mouseketeers contained a paragraph that stated: "Dinner will be served to the Mouseketeers, Jimmie Dodd and Roy Williams, however, due to the lack of space and facilities, it will not be possible to serve the parents and/or guardians in the dining room. However, each parent or guardian will be furnished with 'dinner money.'"

Multiple appearances in the same day were oftentimes scheduled as well. On one such Saturday in 1956, Jimmie, Sharon, Bobby, Lonnie, Annette, and Darlene spent the day crisscrossing Los Angeles and Orange counties for three appearances; first to the Shrine Auditorium in L.A., then to Disneyland, about forty miles south, and then to an elementary school in Pasadena, some forty miles north. A box lunch was provided, to be eaten in the car (their own family car, driven to the locations by a parent or guardian). A note to each Mouseketeer read "Bobby and Sharon: Bring saddle shoes; Annette and Darlene: Bring matching toe shoes; All girls: fix your hair, as no hairdresser will be available."

The wholesome appearance of each Mouseketeer was of utmost importance to the studio. Dave Newell, from the Disney makeup department, would carefully outline the type of makeup they were to wear during public appearances. For the girls, who, like most teenagers, could get carried away with the use of makeup, he specifically indicated to the Disney representative accompanying the group that "the girls have a tendency to 'spot' their rouge and overdo their eye shadow and the lining of their eyes. This gives them a hard and cheap look if not watched closely." They were, therefore, kept in check throughout their hectic schedules.

"I caught on to the popularity of the show when we started doing public appearances," said Karen Pendleton, who was only nine years

The Mouseketeer tour bus surrounded by fans.

old at the time. "It was like 'wow!' But I was so small and so naive I did things that were really dumb. Like when we were told to stop signing autographs, I did that. To this day, I have a guilt complex because there was some man standing there saying, 'Please give me an autograph!' 'I can't, I can't — they told me to stop!'" Karen laughed as she concluded, "I guess I really followed instructions well."

"The studio utilized us one hundred percent of the allowable time," said Tommy Cole. "On weekends we made personal appearances either at Disneyland or other places, sometimes in conjunction with a Disney movie that was opening."

Hospital visits were also occasionally scheduled. For the Mouseketeers, it was perhaps the most difficult part of appearing in public. "They would divide us up to go to the different wards," explained Doreen Tracey. "The first time, it was very hard for me because my mother had had tuberculosis and been in the hospital for four years. So illness was always a fear for me. We just had to go in and shake hands with the kids and smile, but it was hard."

"I would always have a lump in my throat," said Sharon Baird. "But seeing the big grins on their faces was wonderful. So even though it was hard, there was a good part as well. The show touched everyone; it was amazing at how popular it was."

For a while their appearances were strictly local. As their popularity increased, however, the Mouseketeers prepared for a national tour. With their Mouseketeer costumes packed and Disney publicists, casting directors, and parents in tow, the popular young idols of the television screen, along with Jimmie Dodd and Roy Williams, hit the road to meet, greet, and perform. The response was overwhelming.

"Take Portland, for example," recalled Jimmie Dodd. "When we got there we were met by about three thousand kids and their parents at the airport — and yet the time of our arrival was never announced. The day after we left the city, there was the biggest traffic jam in the history of the Portland airport. The rumor had spread that we were due in that day and mobs turned out. I'll never know how the story got out that we were to come back then, because we were already in another city by that time."

The crowds, mirroring the viewership of "The Mickey Mouse Club," were often comprised of many adults in addition to the throngs of kids. "In Houston, several of the Mouseketeers appeared at a big charity show," Jimmie explained. "Ninety percent of the audience were adults! Among the stars who also performed were Dinah Shore and Steve Allen, yet the biggest applause went to the Mouseketeers."

In Oklahoma City, a star-studded program was given in an outdoor amphitheater. As is always the case in a live show, performers must learn to expect the unexpected. In this case, in the middle of "The Mickey Mouse Club" section of the show, Bobby Burgess and Sharon Baird, who were performing, had to contend with a sudden and wind-whipping dust storm.

"We were right down on the plains of Oklahoma at the Oklahoma State Fair," said Bobby. "Then this big windstorm came up and the swirling dust turned our black mouse ears to brown. But nobody in the audience left and we just kept performing. Sharon and I were doing the 'Mousekedance' and Jimmie was playing his guitar. All we could see was what seemed like miles and miles of people out there. I think there were about forty thousand in the audience."

After the show, the Mouseketeers signed autographs as they made their way to their tour bus. One overzealous fan grabbed Bobby's mouse ears right off his head and went racing through the crowd. "Some little guy just pulled them off," Bobby recounted. "We had always been told to take good care of our ears because they had been molded to our heads and weren't easily replaced. So when the kid ran off with mine, Jack Lavin, our casting director, who was with us, ran off the bus and tackled this little kid! The boy was fine, but I got my ears back…and saved fifty bucks!"

"The overwhelming response to our appearances was shocking,"

Flying off to meet and greet.

The "Disney Express" train pulls into a station on its trip across the United States.

said Lonnie Burr. "You'd have thought a President had arrived. I was amazed. We'd get off the plane and there would be thousands of people there. We'd be hustled off into limousines while cops, with sirens blaring, accompanied us to our destination."

All forms of transportation were used to get the Mouseketeers from one place to another. Sometimes planes, sometimes buses, and sometimes railroads. On one such occasion, the children and their parents occupied two private railroad cars on part of their cross-country tour. "It was the 'Disney Express,'" said Sharon Baird. "We slept on the train in upper and lower berths. Parents were on the bottom and kids on top."

"I remember one night, after our parents were asleep, we all sneaked over to Doreen's berth and had a slumber party," said Sharon. "We laughed and giggled just like any kids. During the day, we used to take a portable record player to the observation car, put all the chairs up against the wall, and dance while the train would take us from place to place."

The parents also had their own kind of fun. Sharon's mom, Nicki Baird, recalled: "I remember Joe Funicello, Annette's dad, would mix drinks in the back of the train. He was the bartender. Then everyone would get together and just sit and talk. Nobody overdid, it was just really fun."

Jimmie Dodd also went out on several personal-appearance tours by himself, either to promote a Disney film in theaters at the time or, in conjunction with Talent Round-Up promotions, to draft new talent for the show. His popularity, too, was tremendous and he was always welcomed by huge and enthusiastic crowds of admiring children accompanied by their equally admiring parents. In fact, while Jimmie was on a tour through New England, he was met by such masses of people that it became necessary at nearly every stop to do two shows instead of one to accommodate his devoted fans.

Other incidents included: a department store in New Haven having to stop Jimmie's appearance temporarily because the management was unable to cope with the swarms of children climbing over rails and under barricades in order to get closer to their idol; the Jordan Marsh department store in Boston having to arrange an intricate signaling system so that when the fifth floor (where the appearance was in progress) became crowded to capacity, all escalators were stopped and the elevator operators were instructed to bypass that floor.

For Jimmie, the opportunity to meet the children and parents who watched "The Mickey Mouse Club" was a wonderful one that went beyond mere smiles, autographs, and handshakes. "Being on tour taught me so much about these kids and about people in general," Jimmie said. "They've made the whole show seem different to me. The youngsters are so enthusiastic and the adults so kind. What a fantastically wonderful life they have given me! I hope I never let them down."

Jimmie, forty-six years old in 1956, had been married sixteen years and had no children of his own. One little girl, on learning he wasn't a father, said to him, "Maybe that's why you like children so well." Jimmie quietly responded, "I've always been sorry I had no children. But I can assure you, I have a lot now. And they're all just great."

Everywhere he went, Jimmie could see the influence "The Mickey Mouse Club" had on so many people's lives. "On one flight I made," he said, "a stewardess told me that our TV show had inspired her to take up an airline career. She said she had thought of this kind of job but it wasn't until she saw our 'When I Grow Up' series that she made up her mind. An American Airlines pilot also told me that he makes it a point to see our shows as often as possible, and when he can't, his co-pilot tells him what was on.

"Then," he added, "when I was in Rochester, New York, one night I went to a club to hear George Shearing, the blind jazz musician. George heard I was in the audience and played one of the songs we feature on the show. He told me later he always enjoyed 'The Mickey Mouse Club' and would listen to it whenever possible."

Jimmie's influence even extended to the White House. One of the songs he had written, "Mamie," was penned for Mamie Eisenhower,

JIMMIE DODD

IN PERSON

THURSDAY-SEPTEMBER 12

4:00 p.m.

BIG-LIVE-OUTDOOR
TELECAST

WGEM-TV CHANNEL 10

On the spacious parking lot just
west of Hotel Quincy

JIMMIE **Kroger**

FREE 60,000
TOP VALUE STAMPS
TO BE AWARDED

1st PRIZE 30,000 Top Value Stamps
2nd PRIZE 20,000 Top Value Stamps
3rd PRIZE 10,000 Top Value Stamps

FREE REFRESHMENTS
FREE BALLONS

Added Attractions

**Jackie Bean - Bob Joye
"Toby" Dick Ellis
Possum Holler TV Stars**

Jimmie Dodd often
made his own
"Mickey Mouse Club"
appearances.

First Lady and wife to then President Dwight D. Eisenhower. He wrote Mrs. Eisenhower a letter in January, 1956:

Dear Mrs. Eisenhower:

I hope you remember the redhead who wrote your Fred Waring "Mamie" song, and had the great pleasure of meeting you at that Harlem breakfast in the summer of '52.

Well — this is he — now appearing with Walt Disney's "Mickey Mouse Club" TV show every weekday from 5 to 6 p.m. over ABC. I trust your grandchildren are loyal Mouseketeers, and think they'll enjoy the enclosed recording of our daily theme song.

Also, Mrs. Eisenhower, we would like to, here and now, make you and the President Honorary Mouseketeers. Enclosed you will find your official membership certificates and identification cards.

Welcome, you two wonderful friends, to "The Mickey Mouse Club." God bless you and yours.

Your friend and admirer,
Jimmie Dodd

Bonnie Lynn Fields

Six Mouseketeers had left the show after the 1956 season: Sherry Alberoni, Eileen Diamond, Charley Laney, Larry Larsen, Jay-Jay Solari, and Margene Storey. The youngsters moved on to other show-business opportunities, as with Sherry, who signed to star with Abbott and Costello in their last film together, *Dance with Me, Henry,* or to pursue other activities. In preparation for the 1957 season, they were replaced by four new mice, who were selected through the local Talent Round-Up auditions. "I went to audition to be a guest artist for 'Talent Round-Up Day,'" said Bonnie Lynn Fields. "I was thirteen and I'd been taking dance lessons for a while, but I just started tap six months before. I sang, tap-danced, did some ballet, and they called

Jimmie at his desk at home over which hangs a framed photo of President and Mrs. Eisenhower, along with the sheet music to the song "Mamie," which he wrote for the First Lady.

Don Grady and Linda Hughes
were among the
Mouseketeers selected
to join the show in 1957.

me back for a second audition. Then I went back another time, and they asked me if I'd like to be a Mouseketeer." Having been a faithful viewer of the show in its first two seasons, Bonnie responded, "Are you kidding? Who wouldn't!"

Don Grady, perhaps best known for his role as Robbie Douglas on the long-running television series "My Three Sons," actually began his career as a Mouseketeer. Known then by his real name, Don Agrati, the 13-year-old came to the attention of the Disney Studio when he auditioned for the show in a San Francisco Talent Round-Up and was subsequently flown to Los Angeles to try out. "There were about five hundred kids there," Don recalled. "For my audition, I played four or five different instruments and did a tap dance." He was hired in 1957 to join the club.

"There weren't too many of us that were Mouseketeers, but an awful lot of us wanted to be," said Linda Hughes, who also became a "Mickey Mouse Club" member in 1957. The 10-year-old tap-dancing, baton-twirling ballerina won the coveted role after participating in a local San Diego audition. Lynn Ready, a 12-year-old native of Dallas, Texas, sang, danced, and played the steel guitar and the piano. He was also chosen to become a Mouseketeer that season.

In 1957, "The Mickey Mouse Club" returned to the airwaves with a roster of fourteen Mouseketeers: Sharon Baird, Bobby Burgess, Lonnie Burr, Tommy Cole, Annette Funicello, Darlene Gillespie, Cheryl Holdridge, Cubby O'Brien, Karen Pendleton, Doreen Tracey, Bonnie Lynn Fields, Don

Agrati, Linda Hughes, and Lynn Ready. Added for the viewing audience in this season were new Mouseketeer segments, along with a third "Spin and Marty" serialization, "Clint and Mac," and the 20-episode "Annette" serial.

But this season reflected a dramatic change in format. The hour-long "Mickey Mouse Club" was no longer; the show had been reduced to thirty minutes. In a fact sheet prepared by the Disney Studio, the announcement was made:

> Walt Disney's "Mickey Mouse Club" begins its third consecutive year of entertainment over the ABC-TV Network on September 30 as a five-day-a-week Monday-through-Friday television presentation.
>
> All of the favorite features of the show will be included, though reduced to a half-hour. It will retain the flavor and style of the longer hour-length presentation while giving a faster-paced program. In its new format, "The Mickey Mouse Club" will be seen from 5:30 to 6 p.m. in all time zones.
>
> In general, "The Mickey Mouse Club" will present the Mouseketeers, talented juvenile performers, three times each week with a "Mousekamusical" number or the presentation of a gifted performer in a Talent Round-Up segment. Once a week the program will begin with a Mousecartoon, and once a week with a Mickey Mouse Club Newsreel, presenting various short subjects.
>
> The second part of the 30-minute program will be devoted to the popularly received episodic serials, shown on consecutive days until conclusion. These serials will alternate with continuous Mickey Mouse Club Newsreel Specials. The finales, featuring "Big Mouseketeer" Jimmie Dodd, will be retained, and, of course, the animated "Mickey Mouse Club March" will continue to be an integral part of the show.

Letters poured in to the Disney Studio protesting the change in format as newspapers around the nation reported the story. In one such article, banner-headlined, "Mouseketeer Fans Protest Short Show," an outraged letter stated: "Attention 'Mickey Mouse Club' Fans! It has come to a major crisis! 'The Mickey Mouse Club' is being shortened to a half-hour. Are we going to stand by and see 'Spin and Marty' and all the other serials cut out? We believe something ought to be done!"

Typical of hundreds of letters arriving daily at the studio were:

Add my vehement protest to the proposed cutting of "Mickey Mouse Club" time on television.... With such a dearth of good children's programs, we need you, to educate, entertain properly and inspire our kids.

If you must change the length of "The Mickey Mouse Club," please make it longer. With all the cowboy shows and their killings, bad grammar and cruelty, your show is refreshing, from the talented Mouseketeers to the moral-giving serials to the innocent cartoons or to the educational little messages on closing. When Jimmie tells the kids to stay out of the street, or pick up their toys, they do it.

As a mother, I would like to offer my opinion that it would be a great disappointment to have the Mouseketeer program cut to one-half hour.... It would be hard to express the pleasure the children derive from it. You are building better citizens through it and I hope you will continue this valuable service one hour each weekday.

...Mickey Mouse and Disneyland seem to strike just the right balance, helping the youngster to interpret the world around him and helping him to understand relationships with other human beings.... I would very much regret seeing the show shortened.

To what was this affront to the viewing audience attributed? According to the book *Walt Disney: An American Original*, by Bob Thomas, the reduction in air time was mandated by ABC-TV. He explained, "Despite its immense popularity, 'The Mickey Mouse Club' ran into trouble. ABC claimed it couldn't find enough sponsors who wanted to appeal to the juvenile audience." It was the beginning of the end for Walt Disney's innovative venture into children's television programming.

The 1957–58 season of "The Mickey Mouse Club" was the last to feature new programming. It was, therefore, the end of the series for the Mouseketeers, although the show aired in 1958–59, recut from previous seasons and broadcast three times a week as "The Mickey Mouse Club," on Mondays, Wednesdays, and Fridays from 5:30 to 6 p.m. On Tuesdays and Thursdays, the program aired in the same time period but was called "Adventure Time," featuring reruns of "The Mickey Mouse Club" serials. On September 25, 1959, the final episode was broadcast, and "The Mickey Mouse Club," one of television's most highly rated, award-winning, and praised children's shows went off the air. Why?

At the time, Disney had another hit TV series, "Zorro," which also tied into "The Mickey Mouse Club" cancellation equation. "The 'Zorro' series had been an acknowledged hit for two seasons," explained Thomas in his book, "but ABC declined to renew it. The reason was economic: the network could make more money with series which it owned, rather than those bought from independent producers." The same reasoning applied to "The Mickey Mouse Club."

Apparently, Walt Disney had always considered "The Mickey Mouse Club" to have been a bargain for the network. The cost to produce the one-hour show five times a week and retain a level of quality consistent with Disney standards was very high for the studio. Even with revenue attained from successful merchandise sales, "The Mickey Mouse Club" did not generate high-profit margins for Disney and, as Thomas reported, "Walt believed the network's overloading of commercials caused viewers to lose interest."

The three minutes of commercial time in each 15-minute segment of the hour-long show was divided into three one-minute commercials. In total, there were twelve minutes of commercial announcements in the 60-minute show. Looked at another way, 20 percent of the airtime was devoted to advertising. Viewers indeed recognized the preponderance of commercials and voiced their negative opinions. A letter to Walt Disney from the National Association for Better Radio and Television stated in part:

> As the Evaluation Committee of the National Association for Better Radio and Television, we would like to bring to your attention the various comments — and complaints — that we have had concerning "The Mickey Mouse Club."
>
> "The Mickey Mouse Club" itself is almost universally hailed as "just what we have been looking for" in children's programming. Certainly there is something here for almost every child, both in age and interest. The educational qualities are so skillfully blended with a high level of entertainment that we felt we must express to you, Mr. Disney, our grateful appreciation.
>
> On the other hand, countless parents are protesting to us about the excessive commercialism of this program. The children themselves complain bitterly at the intrusion of so many commercials — clever as they may be — into a program which is otherwise so delightful. Many of these parents feel that the high standards of the program are appreciably lowered by the preponderance of commercials. Therefore, we feel that we can recommend this program only with reservations, despite the excellence of its overall content.
>
> We sincerely hope, Mr. Disney, that you will consider correcting this defect. The good will and appreciation of many, many parents will surely make this a wise move from the sponsors' viewpoint also.

Unfortunately, this was a situation in which Walt Disney had no control; commercial time allowance was dictated by the network. Perhaps Walt was correct in attributing viewers' loss of interest to commercial overload. As Bob Thomas stated in his book, "What killed 'The Mickey Mouse Club'? Walt Disney hinted that it was greed."

"In canceling 'The Mickey Mouse Club' and 'Zorro' series," Thomas further explained, "ABC contended that Disney was barred from offering either of them to other networks. Walt and his brother Roy considered that unfair. They sued ABC, and after a lengthy negotiation, a settlement was reached. Disney would be able to take 'Walt Disney Presents' (the 'Disneyland' show was renamed for its last two seasons on ABC) to another network and would buy out ABC's one-third interest in Disneyland for $7,500,000." But "The Mickey Mouse Club" and "Zorro" were lost, casualties of arbitration.

A 1961 *TV Guide* article reported of Walt's battle with ABC, "The crowning blow came with the demise of 'The Mickey Mouse Club.' Disney used this program as a talent-scout operation to uncover child stars, but he also was proud of its educational features whereby children were taught politics, physiology, safety, etc. A Disney official told me, 'Walt nearly blew his top with ABC because he feels the network choked "The Mickey Mouse Club" to death. First, they jammed it up with commercials. Then, when they couldn't get enough revenue to support the show, they offered it to sponsors indiscriminately. Anyway, it went down the drain.'"

"'The Mickey Mouse Club' had been a brave experiment," Bob Thomas summarized in his book, "an attempt to present important programming to the young television audience. Never again would it be done in commercial television."

By the end of the road, "The Mickey Mouse Club" had amassed an astonishing compendium of interesting facts. For example, 360 original programs were produced; a staff of over 175 (not including performers or musicians) worked on the show: one producer, four associate producers, three general coordinators, eighteen directors, fourteen assistant directors, fifteen cameramen, twenty-three film editors, two special processors, fourteen composers, forty songwriters, one conductor, two sound persons, one re-recording editor, two choreographers, three art directors, thirteen production supervisors, six set directors, one costumer, four makeup people, one facilities coordinator, three production managers, and eleven writers, and from 1955 to 1959 fan mail received reached an astounding figure approaching half a million pieces.

12
NOW IT'S TIME TO SAY GOODBYE

It was good. There's no doubt about it.
"The Mickey Mouse Club" opened
all kinds of doors for me.

— Mouseketeer CUBBY O'BRIEN

FOR THE MOUSEKETEERS, the demise of the show meant the end of going to the studio every day and being with their friends. Sharon Baird recalled her last day on the set. "I cried and cried," she said. "I remember the last thing we had to shoot were happy reaction scenes for 'Circus Day.' Sid Miller would say, 'Okay, now you're seeing something happy and it makes you laugh.' And we would all go, ha, ha, ha, but we were really crying. I'm sure Annette and I used a box of Kleenex that day. It was just terrible. But," she added, "Sid Miller said to us, 'Don't cry, because the more you work in this business, the more you'll be working together again.'"

Many of the Mouseketeers went back to school following the end of filming. But in 1959 and 1960, several of them, along with Jimmie Dodd, went on a personal-appearance tour to Australia where "The Mickey Mouse Club" had been extraordinarily popular. "We were treated like teen idols," said Sharon. "I was about fifteen years old then, and when we got off the airplane there were about five thousand people to meet us. In fact, the crowd broke through the ropes and started rushing toward us and we were told to quickly get back on the plane. Finally, in order to get us through the crowd, they had to roll us on the runway standing on the stairs that were used to disembark the plane."

"While we were there, we were all assigned a bodyguard," Cubby remembered. "Mine was an ex-boxer, a huge guy named Max. I remember that after the shows there would be mobs of people all over the place and Max used to just pick me up by the belt and lift me up over his head and carry me through the people to the limousine."

"They just tore the house down when we went to Australia," Karen added. "I just didn't understand the magnitude of it until then."

"There were so many people waiting for us when we'd finish a show, it was almost impossible to get to the limousine," Sharon said. "And once you were in the car all you could see was a sea of heads. Then the fans would start to rock the car back and forth and the limo driver would just put in it gear and do his best to get through the crowd."

Obviously, there was still a welcome market for "The Mickey Mouse Club." Although Walt Disney was not able to bring the show to another network, his ownership of the series allowed the studio to rebroadcast the program in syndication, which they did from 1962 to 1965 and 1975 to 1976 in the half-hour format. The cost of the original show was estimated at about $14,000,000. At the time of syndication, the same talent and expenses would have put the show cost at about $22,000,000. An estimated 280 hours were used for the syndication, with several new features added to the show to give it freshness. The

By the end of the series, the Mouseketeers had very much matured even though they were still attending school in the little red trailer. Pictured (from left to right; top row) Bobby and Mrs. Seaman; (middle row) Sharon, Cubby, Doreen, and Jimmie; (bottom row) Karen and Cheryl.

Disney Studio bore its own expenses for film processing, editing, new materials, and merchandising. Also, the show was designed and edited so that local announcers were able to use commercials and announcements for their particular audiences. Interestingly, by 1962, in the seven years that had passed since the 1955 launch of the show, 30,000,000 more children had been born, creating a whole new audience for the syndicated series.

Based on the program's initial popularity, by the time "The Mickey Mouse Club" was in syndication, over 500,000 more mouse-eared hats had been sold. In the first year of syndication, the estimated audience approximated 12,000,000 children daily and the program reached every major market in the United States. While the show was in syndication, Jimmie Dodd and Mickey Mouse continued to tour the country to promote the show. In 1963, the second year of syndication, the show still had 10,000,000 viewers.

The foreign distribution of "The Mickey Mouse Club" went well beyond the initial years of syndication. Because of the various broadcasting rules and regulations that governed each country, the show was distributed either by being sold outright to stations and financed by local sponsorship, or, if the stations were government-owned, being sold to the government agency. Wherever possible, dubbing of translations in the foreign tongue was used and segments were shown with new audio in Spanish, French, German, Italian, and Japanese. Overall, eighteen countries around the world aired "The Mickey Mouse Club" from 1958 to 1970. From April 1983 to February 1989 the Disney Channel broadcast the original shows, and in 1994 Walt Disney Home Video released a ten-volume set of the "best" of the original "Mickey Mouse Club."

By 1960, all "Mickey Mouse Club" activities had ceased for the Mouseketeers. They rejoined the outside world as individuals who had come together in childhood as a group, an exclusive fraternity consisting of thirty-nine original members. Each would take a different path, although their lives would continue to commingle. And the memories of "The Mickey Mouse Club" would continue to endure.

Directly after his stint on the show, Mouseketeer Lonnie Burr completed his senior year in high school and went on to college. "When I finished the series, I didn't want to do any more shows," he said. "I wanted to grow up. I tried to be Cary Grant, but instead I was this guy with ears." At the time, "Being a Mouseketeer was not exactly what I wanted my image to be," he remarked. "I really enjoyed the experience, but as a young man I just wasn't mature enough to realize the value of things."

After earning both a bachelor's and a master's degree in theater, Burr tried his hand once again at performing. "I started back in show business and couldn't get anything at all for three or four years," he said. "I sold real estate, taught jazz and tap, sold men's clothes, and was a bar manager. Eventually, I did several films and a few TV shows. But I had to fight the Mouseketeer image with casting people. They wanted me to tap-dance with ears, you know. I'd say, 'No. I'm twenty years old, I'm an actor.'"

Lonnie appeared in the national company of *George M* in 1970 and moved to New York where he resided for five years. "I did mostly Broadway and off-Broadway and I started doing more writing," he reported. His written work resulted in several national poetry awards. Additionally, he wrote a number of plays and contributed articles to a variety of publications, including the *Village Voice*, the Los Angeles *Times* and *American Film* magazine.

In 1978, Simon & Schuster published Burr's book, *Two for the Show: Great Comedy Teams (1898–1978)*. Since that time, Lonnie has divided his time between the written word and performing. "I've acted in over forty Equity plays including *Tamara* and *42nd Street*, and about twenty-five films, most recently *Hook, Mr. Saturday Night*, and *Newsies*. Lonnie has also made numerous television appearances and guested on a variety of radio and TV talk shows. His many writing credits encompass magazine and newspaper as well as TV and radio.

"I wrote an obituary once that said 'Lonnie Burr, former Mouseketeer, scaled the Matterhorn, was the best Hamlet in his time and wrote the best novel of the late 20th century.' So, Mouseketeer will always come first," he said. "Whatever you do. That used to bother me a great deal, along with becoming a generic. You know, except for Annette, we were 'the Mouseketeers.' But now I thought, why not just be happy and enjoy what's there?"

Following "The Mickey Mouse Club," Sharon Baird completed her high school education and then went on to college. "When I got out of school, I worked as a full-time secretary," she explained. "Then after I got married, my husband and I toured the nightclub circuit with an act called 'Two Cats and a Mouse.'" Because of her small stature (4 feet 9 inches tall), Sharon then went on to a successful career performing in children's shows, both onstage and on television, portraying a variety of costumed characters. She appeared in such programs as "Lidsville," "H.R. Pufnstuf," "Land of the Lost," and "The New Zoo Revue."

Returning to her Disney roots, Sharon starred in several Disney Channel children's series, including "Welcome to Pooh Corner" and "Dumbo's Circus." She also starred in the feature film *Ratboy*, worked as a children's acting coach on TV comedy series, and appeared onstage with comedian Gallagher, as well as being featured on his videotape, "Over Your Head." Divorced, Sharon currently resides in Reno, Nevada. She continues to maintain a close relationship with the other Mouseketeers, particularly with Annette, who still remains her best friend.

"I went back to my senior year in high school and just tried to get back to normal," explained Bobby Burgess. "The only strange thing was that I would walk down the hall at Poly High in Long Beach and they would say, 'Hi, Mickey!' — that kind of thing. But that was

Bobby had danced with his future "Lawrence Welk Show" partner, Barbara Boylan, on a "Talent Round-Up Day."

fine. Then I went to college after that and got into a fraternity and made a lot of friends who are still my friends today. When I was nineteen, I got on 'The Lawrence Welk Show.'

"I had danced with a girl named Barbara Boylan," Bobby added, "and had won a scholarship to her dancing school. We teamed up just for fun, doing ballroom dancing. On 'The Mickey Mouse Club' I mostly did tap, jazz, a little ballet, a little folk, and some singing, but with Barbara it was ballroom. All during 'The Mickey Mouse Club,' I was dancing with Barbara on the side. As a matter of fact, when she was fourteen, she appeared on the show in a 'Talent Round-Up Day' with me."

It was as a result of winning a dance contest that Bobby and Barbara landed an appearance on "The Lawrence Welk Show." "We danced to 'Calcutta,' a big hit song at the time, and they really loved it. So they invited us to come back week after week for about six months. Finally, on the air, Lawrence Welk announced that we would be regulars. Although Barbara left the show after a few years, I stayed on with different dancing partners for twenty-one years, until he stopped producing original shows.

"I loved working on the Welk show," Bobby said, with his broad trademark smile. "It was completely creative. I did all my own choreography, planned the camera shots, wardrobe, and sets. It was great. In fact, I used a lot of steps in my work that I learned as a Mouseketeer. And, believe it or not, Lawrence had no written contracts. If you did a good job, he kept you on. As long as you didn't drink on the job and you were on time, that's about all he asked." Bobby's previous history at Disney had taught him well how to be and act as a professional.

He recognized that: "Disney just kind of laid a great foundation to know how to be a professional. I mean, we couldn't touch the props, we couldn't eat in our costumes, we had to know our dances. For me, it was a great moral beginning or something. I felt like I needed to live up to the reputation of being a Mouseketeer and representing Walt Disney."

In 1971, Bobby married Kristie Floren, daughter of Myron Floren, the Welk show's resident accordionist. "Because of the show, I had known her since she was nine," Bobby said of his wife, who is ten years his junior. "We have four children: Becki, seventeen; Robert, fifteen; Wendi, eleven; and Brent, who is seven." The family lives in the Hollywood Hills, and Bobby still dances for a living, traveling with either his current dancing partner, Elaine Niverson, or with "The Stars of the Lawrence Welk Show," performing around the country at state fairs, theaters-in-the-round, and in special engagements. Moving almost directly from "The Mickey Mouse Club" to "The Lawrence Welk Show," Bobby observed, was "real lucky. I went from one family institution right into another."

"The Lawrence Welk Show" provided the platform for yet another Mouseketeer to launch his adult career. "I was about thirteen when I auditioned for Lawrence Welk, who was putting together a junior band," recalled Cubby O'Brien. "Bobby wasn't on the show yet when I got the job. The junior band concept only lasted about six months, but I stayed with the show as a musician doing specialty numbers for about two years. From there, I did some acting in commercials and did some TV shows like 'Zane Grey Theater' and 'Cheyenne,' but I was a drummer and that's what I really wanted to do."

Cubby decided to pursue that goal and began by joining small bands around Los Angeles and playing local lounges. "Then I met Spike Jones, and worked with his band for about two years before he passed away," Cubby said. "The experience I got with Spike's band led to drumming for a lot of famous acts. I worked with Ann-Margret on her first nightclub act in Harrah's at Lake Tahoe. I traveled with her on and off for a couple of years, which led to joining the orchestras of several TV shows. I was a regular on 'The Jim Nabors Show' for a while and then did 'The Carol Burnett Show' for six and a half years.

Toward the end of my stint on the Burnett show, I met the Carpenters [singing brother and sister act] when they were guests on the program."

That meeting was to prove fortuitous for Cubby. "They asked me to go on tour with them and I ended up staying for ten years. We did many TV specials, and I recorded and traveled with them several times to Europe and Japan," he said. "It was very nice." Cubby went on to work with a variety of topflight performers such as Juliet Prowse, Debbie Reynolds, Steve Lawrence and Eydie Gorme, Lena Horne, Diana Ross, Joel Grey, Bernadette Peters, Andy Williams, and, for several years of late, touring with Shirley MacLaine. In fact, during Shirley MacLaine's act, she introduces Cubby as her drummer and as a former Mouseketeer, inviting him to do a tap dance to "Bye, Bye, Blues."

"Depending on where we're traveling and how popular 'The Mickey Mouse Club' was in that region, whether in the States or in places around the world like Australia and Africa, people go crazy. I often get requests for newspaper, radio, and TV interviews. Everybody seems to remember 'The Mickey Mouse Club.'"

Divorced, Cubby has a 25-year-old daughter, Alicia, and is now married to a former flight attendant he met in Las Vegas during his tenure with the Carpenters. He and his wife, Terry, reside in a small town in Texas, just outside of Dallas where she grew up. "We used to live in the San Fernando Valley," Cubby explained, "but I was away on the road so much it made more sense for us to live closer to Terry's family." Cubby's busy schedule keeps him traveling most of the year doing what he loves best, sitting behind a set of drums just as he did on "The Mickey Mouse Club."

Cubby's on-screen childhood partner, Karen Pendleton, remembers life after "The Mickey Mouse Club." "I didn't stay in show business," she said. "Working at Disney was like being with your family.

But going on auditions after the show ended — well, I tried it for a while, but I just felt really uncomfortable. It was scary. And you have to be really assertive when you're in show business. I wasn't. I just happened to do my little dance and got chosen to be on the show. I was not primed to be in show business.

"But 'The Mickey Mouse Club' was a very positive experience for me," she admitted. "Although when I went back to public school, it was really awful because I didn't know a lot of people there. I had been isolated with this wonderful little studio family for four years. In public school, the kids were so mean! 'Wiggle your ears, we'll give you some cheese,' they would say. The first day I was there, all the kids crowded around me at lunchtime. My mother said to always be pleasant, so I really tried to be nice. But I was scared. They'd ask me for an autograph and then they'd tear it up.

"One day," she continued, "a kid came by and cut my hair with scissors. Another one threw a worm in my mouth. All through junior high I got nothing but teasing. By the time I got to high school, it didn't bother me anymore. But it was a really traumatic experience."

Karen, who is divorced, has a daughter, Staci, twenty years old, who attends college in Fresno, California, where she and Karen reside. Living a quiet life in central California, Karen's world was turned upside down in 1983 when tragedy struck. "I was in an automobile accident," Karen related. "My spine was irreparably injured and it left me permanently paralyzed from the waist down."

In the struggle to pick up the pieces and regain control of her life, which from that point on was confined to a wheelchair, Karen has made a remarkable and admirable recovery. "After my accident, I went back to college and got a bachelor's degree in psychology," she explained. "I'm going to start my master's degree in counseling, plus I'm working full-time for a battered-women's shelter." How does she view the fate that life has dealt her? "More good has come from it than bad," she said. "I'm involved on the board of the California Association of the Physically Handicapped, I have a beautiful daughter, and my life is very full."

Doreen Tracey worked as a performer following her tenure on "The Mickey Mouse Club," spending several years in Vietnam during the war. "I didn't go there as a Mouseketeer," she explained. "I went there as a rock 'n' roller with my own show. Then word got out that Mouseketeer Doreen was in the country. I would have shows with maybe fifteen hundred soldiers in the audience and at the end of my act inevitably someone would shout, 'Doreen, please, we want you to sing "The Mickey Mouse Club" song!' Then they would all stand up and we'd sing together, 'Now, it's time to say goodbye…' like it was 'The Star-Spangled Banner' or something. It was very powerful because it was so American."

Considering herself "the rebellious black sheep of the Mouseketeers," Doreen moved in and out of show business while raising her son, Bradley, now thirty-two years old. She worked as one of many advisers on *Apocalypse Now,* and has written a manuscript based on her life and Vietnam experiences, which she is hoping to publish. She is divorced and currently works as Manager of Operations at an entertainment company in Hollywood. Meantime, she continues to do a great deal of writing in her spare time. But her show-business ancestry that began with her vaudevillian parents lives on. "My mom, Bessie, is still doing her act," she said, with a big smile. "She's ninety years old and performing as a Sunshine Girl for the senior citizens of Burbank."

What can be said about Annette that the world doesn't already know? She came into our lives and into our hearts in 1955 and still dwells there today, some forty years later. "People always ask me, 'Why were you the most popular?'" she said. "My only answer is timing. I guess it was just my time." Annette was the only Mouseketeer kept under contract to Disney following the demise of "The Mickey

Mouse Club," and went on to appear in a number of television shows including "Zorro" and "Elfego Baca," as well as starring in the Disney feature films *The Shaggy Dog, Babes in Toyland, The Misadventures of Merlin Jones*, and *The Monkey's Uncle*.

A successful recording career also coincided with Annette's acting chores. Her singles, including "Tall Paul," "First Name Initial," "How Will I Know My Love?" and "Pineapple Princess," topped the recording charts. Her career flourishing, the versatile performer went on to work for American International Pictures and star in a string of successful Beach Party movies with Frankie Avalon including *Beach Party, Beach Blanket Bingo, Muscle Beach Party*, and *How to Stuff a Wild Bikini*, among others.

In 1965, Annette married, interrupting her busy career schedule to raise a family. "I have three children," she said, "Gina, born in 1965, my son Jackie, born in 1970, and Jason, born in 1974. After each child, I gave up the business for several years, slowly getting back into it each time. I feel very fortunate that I was able to successfully return."

Annette, who has divorced and remarried, still remains a very family-oriented person. "I'm a homebody," she admitted. "I avoid Hollywood parties like the plague. I much prefer spending the time with my parents, my husband, and my children."

Not only associated with movies, television, and records, Annette has also been a popular television spokeswoman for several well-known products. "I loved doing commercials because it required a minimum amount of time away from home," she said. "I was spokeswoman for Mennen baby products for three years, did a hair commercial, and represented Skippy peanut butter for ten years."

In 1987, Annette teamed once again with her Beach Party buddy, Frankie Avalon, to co-produce and star in Paramount Pictures' *Back to the Beach*, a tongue-in-cheek comedy pairing the famous duo as parents of two worrisome teenagers. A year-long "Frankie and Annette" concert tour followed in 1989 and 1990, which featured nostalgic live performances by the pair recalling the popular Beach Party music of the '60s, along with performances of their respective chart-topping hit songs of that era.

In July 1992 Annette's idyllic life took a serious turn when she publicly disclosed that she was battling multiple sclerosis, a crippling disease of the central nervous system. Since that time, the public outpouring of love and support has been overwhelming, while the disease continues to rob Annette of her ability to walk or sign her name or read a book. She is, however, a fighter who refuses to surrender to adversity. "I think you only have two choices in this kind of situation. Either you give in to it or you fight it. I intend to fight."

Serving as a role model for disabled people throughout the world, Annette continues to remain in the public eye and has pledged to help others by creating the Annette Funicello Research Fund for Neurological Diseases, to benefit a broad spectrum of neurological disorders. And, as testament to her positive attitude toward life, she continues to broaden her horizons through many endeavors, including the successful Annette Funicello Teddy Bear Company and her involvement in numerous business ventures. Undoubtedly, she has retained that undefined quality that set her apart so many years ago.

"I finished high school at Hollywood Professional School after the end of 'The Mickey Mouse Club,'" said Tommy Cole. "When I left the Mouseketeers, I went from the 'A' list of parties to 'Tommy who?' All child actors go through that when the limelight stops. As a teenager, everybody recognized me, I signed autographs, people were in awe of me. The next minute, nobody could remember my name and I couldn't *buy* a job."

Despite this rude awakening, Tommy managed to keep a level head about the situation. "I still had my friends in the neighborhood and my friends at school," he recalled. "I was just sort of floundering in finding my niche. I still sang and I still went out on interviews, but I didn't get many parts as an actor. I did better as a singer, although still typecast as one of those kids with the ears on." Tommy did appear, however, on several TV shows, including "Leave It To Beaver" and "My Three Sons" as well as being featured in the Disney film *Westward Ho, The Wagons!*

The singing Mouseketeer then toured the country for a number of years with various rock-'n'-roll groups as well as with popular vocalist Johnny Mathis. Then he decided to make an unusual career change. "Although I had spent almost sixteen years as a performer, there were times when it was difficult to pay the bills," he said. "So I decided to try something else." In 1966, Tommy moved behind the camera and became a makeup artist. "I knew the basics of makeup from being an actor," he commented. "But I also did a lot of observing and practicing and, thank God, I've been very successful."

Tommy's first job in makeup was with the ABC Television Network where he spent several years. In 1968, he became a staff makeup artist at NBC and remained with the network until 1976, when he decided it would be more lucrative to become a free-lancer. Indeed, he hasn't stopped working since, and has become one of Hollywood's most sought after makeup professionals and the recipient of an Emmy Award for his work on the highly acclaimed mini-series "Backstairs at the White House." Tommy has been makeup artist for Cher, Barbara Walters, and Raquel Welch, among many others, in addition to working on such shows as "Designing Women," "Evening Shade," and "Wings." He also works in commercials and feature films.

Tommy and his wife, Aileen, have two children, 17-year-old daughter Lindsay and 15-year-old son Casey, and live in Sherman Oaks, California, only a few miles from the Disney Studio.

Pigtailed Mouseketeer Darlene Gillespie completed high school at Providence High in Burbank following "The Mickey Mouse Club." "I did a little television and even sang in Las Vegas for a while," she said. "But I was married and didn't like the unpredictability of show business, so I went back to school and got my degree in nursing."

Actually, it was quite natural for her to do so since everyone in Darlene's family is in either medicine, law, or show business.

Darlene has two children, Lisa, twenty-three, and David, twenty-one. She is divorced and continues to work in southern California as a nurse, and is often still recognized in her uniform.

"'The Mickey Mouse Club' has been through different cycles, different generations," Darlene said. "When the show was syndicated on television I never told my children that the pigtailed girl named Darlene was their mom. I thought perhaps it would embarrass them or that they would think the show silly. Finally, one of my neighbors told my children that Mouseketeer Darlene was their mother. Luckily, they liked the show and were very proud of me. That made it all worthwhile."

Other notable graduates of "The Mickey Mouse Club" who continued their show-business careers included Paul Petersen ("The Donna Reed Show"), Don Grady ("My Three Sons"), Johnny Crawford ("The Rifleman"), and Sherry Alberoni (motion pictures *The Three Worlds of Gulliver* and *Dance with Me, Henry,* among others, plus numerous TV appearances and voice-overs for many Saturday morning cartoon stars). The rest of the group went on to successful careers in a variety of industries and only one original Mouseketeer, Mike Smith, who was part of the group in 1955–56, is deceased.

As for the two adult leaders of "The Mickey Mouse Club," Jimmie Dodd continued to work as an entertainer, along with his wife, Ruth, until his sudden and untimely death in Hawaii in 1964. Roy Williams, the Big Mooseketeer, worked for the Disney organization for many years following the end of the show until retirement. On November 7, 1976, he too passed away.

"The Mickey Mouse Club" went off the air in its initial run in 1959. But did the Mouseketeers ever really go away? They came back in syndication in the '60s and '70s. In 1977–78, Disney syndicated "The New Mickey Mouse Club," starring twelve talented kids in a slick

Jimmie Dodd and Roy Williams, the leaders of the club.

Vegas-like version of the show that never really got off the ground. In 1978, to celebrate "Mickey's 50th," several of the new Mouseketeers appeared in a Disneyland show with original mice Tommy, Lonnie, Sharon, and Cubby.

Then, in 1980, a new resurgence of interest in the original group took place when a national media search was launched by the Disney Studio to locate the thirty-nine "Mickey Mouse Club" members who had appeared on the '50s show. They were being sought to don their ears once again for the TV cameras, this time as adults and in full color, to star in the 25th reunion of the Mouseketeers on an NBC-TV network special.

13

THE
25TH REUNION
AND BEYOND

I guess being a Mouseketeer is like riding a bicycle.
Once you learn how to do it right, you never forget.

— PAUL WILLIAMS, host of "The Mouseketeer
Reunion," November 23, 1980

.

BIG CHEESES AT DISNEY HUNT FOR MISSING MOUSEKETEERS,"
declared a banner New York newspaper headline. "The people at
Walt Disney Studio have done everything but call in the Hardy Boys
to find four missing members of the original 'Mickey Mouse Club'
cast," the story reported. "So far, Disney has located thirty-five original Mouseketeers for a 25th anniversary TV reunion special. Because
the show goes into rehearsal next month, Disney is now appealing to
the press for help in tracking down the missing four. They are: Larry

"Mickey Mouse Club" director Sid Miller and Annette Funicello reunite on the set of "The Mouseketeer Reunion" show.

Larsen, Charley Laney, Ronnie Steiner, and Don Underhill. All are now in their mid- to late-thirties."

The Disney "all points bulletin" issued to the press created pre-show "Mickey Mouse Club" publicity made in heaven as TV, radio, and newspapers all over the country carried the story on the Mouseketeer manhunt. In days, the media blitz paid off — the missing mice had been found. "Charley Laney, Larry Larsen, Don Underhill and Ronnie Steiner called the Walt Disney Studio in Burbank after hearing the news reports of the search," reported the press.

"I believe they found the last one at 5 p.m. last night," said Jan Jorgenson, a secretary at the Disney Studio in a newspaper interview. "I heard a shriek down the hall and that was what it was." The four Mouseketeers, each of whom had been on the show just one season, were listed as missing when they failed to turn up for a Mouseketeer reunion at Disneyland honoring Mickey's 50th birthday two years earlier. It turned out that three of the four were living in Disneyland's backyard. Larry Larsen, an engineer, lived about fifteen miles from the Park; Don Underhill, a credit manager, was employed by an Orange County (the county where Disneyland is located) company; and Charley Laney was a supermarket manager in the San Diego area. Ronnie Steiner checked in with Disney all the way from Winnipeg, Manitoba, in Canada.

Rehearsals for "The Mouseketeer Reunion," began at the Dis-

Twenty-six of the thirty-one original Mouseketeers who appeared on the "Reunion."

ney Studio on July 10, 1980, with thirty-one of the original Mouseke-teers participating in the show. Then, after nearly two weeks of rehearsals, and just days before taping the show, the Hollywood Screen Actors Guild union went on strike, shutting down production of "The Mouseketeer Reunion" for three months.

Finally, in late October 1980, before an invited audience, the Mouseketeers, ranging in age from thirty-three to forty-one, had the rare opportunity to sing and dance together again, just as they had twenty-five years earlier. Not only were they performing on the same Disney soundstage as they had as children, but draped behind them was the original Mouseketeer curtain, hauled out of 21-year storage, newly cleaned and in perfect condition. "It sent a chill up my spine," said Sharon Baird. "How many people get to go back twenty-five years, be in exactly the same place and see exactly the same faces? I guess that must be what nostalgia is."

"I never recognized this before," said Lonnie Burr, "but we are a family. It feels good to be part of this continuity." Tommy Cole added, "Where else could I get recognized at the age of thirty-eight for something I did twenty-five years ago," while Darlene Gillespie jokingly moaned of the hard work involved in performing again, "Everything hurts."

The show was hosted by singer-songwriter Paul Williams, who had actually auditioned to become a Mouseketeer as a child. High-lights of the reunion included a split screen in which several Mouseke-teers were shown as they appeared in the 1950s programs and as they appeared on the reunion show, singing and dancing to the same musi-cal number with themselves, then and now. The program also includ-ed "Anything Can Happen Day," with the Mouseketeers singing, "I Wish I Were a Kid Again" and describing their feeling about the era in which the original show aired. Also featured was a medley of songs by Jimmie Dodd and a "Talent Round-Up Day" segment highlighted by a visit from Tim Considine, star of "Spin and Marty" and "The

Annette and Bobby try out an old dance routine.

Hardy Boys" serials. The closing of the show, of course, was tradi-tional: "Now it's time to say goodbye to all our company, M-I-C ["See ya real soon"], K-E-Y ["Why, because we *like* you!"], M-O-U-S-E!"

Airing on November 23, 1980, as part of "Disney's Wonderful World," on NBC-TV, "The Mouseketeer Reunion" received some interesting reviews.

Variety's critique of the show stated, in part:

A marvelous evening of nostalgia, the 25th anniversary reunion of the original Mouseketeers must have found many viewers reflecting in a bittersweet manner of the rapid passage of time. For anyone who grew up in the 1950s, watching the former kiddie stars singing and dancing side-by-side with clips of themselves as kids was as poignant as reading Roger Kahn's book about the Brooklyn Dodgers of the '50s, *The Boys of Summer*.

It's not that the Mouseketeers have become seedy and decrepit. On the contrary, they're still an unusually peppy and healthy-looking bunch for the most part, a tribute to Disney's taste and judgment.

Other reviews reported:

The faces are lined, some hairlines are receding and some have gray in their hair. But what do you expect? They haven't been teenagers for quite a while and now most of them are in their thirties and some must be in their early forties. But no matter, "The Mouseketeer Reunion" is a fine bit of nostalgia for all of us who remember the original "Mickey Mouse Club."

If you were a kid in 1955, "The Mickey Mouse Club" was *the* event to look forward to after school each day. Funny, but despite the years, I still remember the words to the song…and maybe you will, too.

— *The Register*

Thirty-one grown-up Mouseketeers sprouted silver ears on "Disney's Wonderful World" on NBC for the 25th anniversary of "The Mickey Mouse Club." Any child of the '50s wondered: Could this troupe of middle-aged ex-child television heroes compete with cherished memories of the Mouseketeers?…Walt Disney would have been proud.

After an hour of spirited nostalgia, the Mouseketeers tenderly entoned the mournful "Now it's time to say goodbye...." It was more than the end of a program. Recess was over for a children's world that successfully had been recreated, then celebrated, by adults who had been there.

— Los Angeles *Times*

Riding the coattails of the successful "Mouseketeer Reunion," and the revival of interest in the group, there seemed to be a great opportunity, from the Disney Studio's standpoint, to involve some of the original Mouseketeers in a variety of Disney shows and events. Not only would the baby boomers of the '50s be able to meet their onetime idols, but the involvement of the Mouseketeers in these activities would create tremendous publicity and give the former mouse-eared stars a chance to once again step into the limelight.

The first such event, in which four Mouseketeers (Sharon Baird, Tommy Cole, Sherry Alberoni, and Lonnie Burr) became involved, was a salute to Disney on television, called "Disneyvision," presented at New York's Museum of Broadcasting (now the Museum of Radio and Television) in August and September of 1981. The Disney television festival included public screenings of a variety of Disney TV programming. The weeks of the event were divided into categories: Fantasy Week, Nature and Science Week, Western Week, Week of Specials, and Mouseketeer Week. The four Mouseketeers enjoyed tremendous positive response to their appearance at the museum.

For their time in New York, a slate of publicity had been arranged. They appeared at "Mickey Mouse Club Day" at Shea Stadium, along with Mickey Mouse, who threw out the first ball of a New York Mets baseball game. They also appeared as guests on TV and radio programs and participated in newspaper interviews. It was kind of like the old days.

The newfound popularity of the grown-up Mouseketeers led to

a "Mouseketeer Reunion Show," staged for several years on fall weekends at Disneyland during the early- and mid-1980s. Mouseketeers Bobby, Tommy, Lonnie, Cubby, Don, Sharon, Sherry, Darlene, and Bonnie headlined the shows (although not all appeared in all shows), which nostalgically re-created the format of the original "Mickey Mouse Club." With the success of each Disneyland appearance, the show itself became more embellished and elaborately staged, with performances eight times each weekend for several weeks. The fast-paced 35-minute production included sixteen musical numbers, numerous costume changes, and incorporated a dozen Disney characters into the proceedings.

"I went to the gym six days a week for three months to prepare for each show," Tommy Cole remarked. "I'm sort of a middle-aged mouse, but I had a ball at Disneyland. I'm an old ham and I love the applause. We'd be out onstage playing to a full house, who were applauding us with tears in their eyes because they remember and have this nostalgia — this feeling for you, the feeling of being friends even though they didn't know you. Let's face it, I still love wearing my ears."

"I remember a couple of times saying to the other Mouseketeers in the show, 'Do you guys feel a little strange wearing these hats?' " Bobby admitted. "But then I would think of Jimmie and say to myself, no, I'm representing something special to the parents and the kids out there."

"It was amazing to hear the entire audience singing along," said Mouseketeer Sherry Alberoni. "We weren't just getting audiences in our own age group, but we were crossing three generations: parents who were the kids of the '50s, grandparents who were the parents then, and kids who were watching the reruns on the Disney Channel."

"I loved the dancing," said Sharon Baird, of the Disneyland shows. "And we knew each other's moves so well because of the years we had spent doing exactly the same thing as kids." With the success

The nine Mouseketeers who starred on "The Mouseketeer Reunion."

of the Disneyland shows, the Mouseketeers were thrown into the spotlight with all its attendant duties: more TV, radio, and newspaper interviews, meet and greets, autograph signings, etc. They were having a blast.

Mouseketeers Karen Pendleton, Cheryl Holdridge, and Larry Larsen also participated during one such Disneyland reunion, although they did not appear onstage in the show, but, rather, took part in the Magic Kingdom parade as well as signing autographs for Park guests. "After I had my accident and we did the 1985 appearance at Disneyland (celebrating the 30th anniversary of the Mouseketeers), I think that's when the impact of the show really hit me all over again," Karen recalled. "We signed autographs and all these grown-up people, like groupies, would come and wait in line to meet us. I was shocked. Maybe that's because for the first time in my life after my accident, I really got in touch with myself and realized what this was all about. How neat this was and how special I felt to have been part of the whole 'Mickey Mouse Club' thing. It's like being a professional football coach. There's only but so many of them in the whole world."

Adding to their live performance repertoire, several of the same Mouseketeers were showcased in 1987, 1989, and 1990 at the world-famous Hollywood Bowl as part of "The Disney Symphonic Spectacular." This was a singing and dancing musical extravaganza with dazzling production numbers that featured a host of performers and well-known Disney characters; the evening shows played to sold-out audiences of over 17,000 per night. For the Mouseketeers, it was more than just a show; it was déjà vu. They had been there before, over thirty years earlier, on Saturday, August 11, 1956, on "Family Night at the Hollywood Bowl."

In 1988, in conjunction with Mickey Mouse's 60th birthday, which was celebrated throughout The Walt Disney Company, two original Mouseketeers, Bobby and Sherry, were heavily involved as Disney spokespeople in the publicity campaign to promote the event.

All grown up but still dancing to "Fun with Music."

They traveled that year to cities that included New York, Washington, D.C., Philadelphia, Boston, Detroit, Chicago, Orlando, Kansas City, Denver, Salt Lake City, Seattle, Portland, San Francisco, Dallas, San Antonio, and New Orleans, among others. They also had the opportunity to visit Alaska and Hawaii as well as touring in Sydney and Melbourne, Australia, and in Auckland, New Zealand.

The New York City celebration of Mickey's 60th, in August of 1988, was quite an elaborate affair. The city was special to the famous mouse, since he had made his motion picture debut in "Steamboat Willie," at New York's Colony Theater (now the Broadway Theater). The festivities were staged at South Street Seaport where Bobby and Sherry were joined by Mickey himself, along with New York City Mayor Ed Koch and Disney Company vice-chairman, Roy Disney. Amid much media madness, Mickey and the mayor released 4,000 balloons to kick off the party, and ended up on the front page of the New York *Daily News*. The photo caption read: "When little Eddie Koch was three, a cartoon mouse made his screen debut in 'Steamboat Willie.' Now both these chaps have achieved a measure of fame, and both were in fine form yesterday at Pier 17 at South Street Seaport, where Mickey Mouse was taking part in celebrations of his 60th birthday."

Many publicity and promotional events featuring Bobby and Sherry, along with those that also headlined Tommy, Lonnie, Sharon and Bonnie, filled much of 1988. Then, in 1989, The Disney Channel invited Annette, Bobby, Sharon, Don, Tommy, and Sherry to guest-star on the first anniversary of their updated version of "The Mickey Mouse Club," which debuted on The Disney Channel in April 1989.

Videotaped before a live studio audience of teenagers at the Disney/MGM Studios in Orlando, Florida, the half-hour contemporary "Mickey Mouse Club" stars a group of talented young people, ages eleven to fifteen, who sing, dance, and do comedy, although they no longer sprout black circular ears atop their heads. Stephen Fields, formerly senior vice-president of original programming for The Disney Channel, remarked at the series debut, "Just as the original 'Mickey Mouse Club' helped define the 1950s, we believe the new show will become an important part of the culture of the 1990s. We think we've developed something that's exciting, that young people throughout America will identify with." The show has indeed become one of the most watched series by older children (pre-teens and teens) on The Disney Channel.

Lonnie Burr, Sharon Baird, and Sherry Alberoni look on as Mickey Mouse throws out the first ball of the game at New York's Shea Stadium.

But remnants and memories of the original show survive, both in reality and in the minds and hearts of the millions who grew up on the show. The Walt Disney Archives houses the reality, maintaining original files, photos, and the few props and costumes that still exist: Jimmie's Mousegetar, donated to the Archives by his wife, Ruth, after his death; Annette's name shirt and Talent Round-Up costume. But the memories — they live on in us, no matter how much time has passed.

Looking back, the Mouseketeers pondered the popularity of the show, what it meant to them, and why people were still interested

The 1980's Disneyland show starring Mouseketeers (from left to right) Sharon, Cubby, Sherry, Lonnie, Bonnie, Tommy, along with Disney stars Minnie Mouse, Mickey Mouse, and Donald Duck.

forty years later. "They knew it was good, wholesome family entertainment," Bobby observed. "It had the stamp of Walt Disney on it and the whole family could watch it; they wouldn't be offended in any way. Also, for the most part we weren't precocious show-biz kids. We were the kids next door. That's why so many children could relate to us."

Lonnie agreed. "The majority of the kids were not professionals," he said. "If someone would sing off-key, they left it in. The audience would see that the Mouseketeers were not perfect kids, and they felt they could do what the Mouseketeers could do. Another important factor is that we weren't kids playing a role. We were kids playing ourselves, and there were no others like that on television at the time. As an adult, the best thing about the show is, unless somebody is trying to be a pseudo-faux-sophisticate and a cynical curmudgeon of some kind, almost everybody responds positively to 'The Mickey Mouse Club.'"

"In the old days, I'd be very shy about letting people know I was a Mouseketeer," Doreen confessed. "Now I never hide it. I just say, 'Yep, that's who I am,' and they'll say, 'You were really a Mouseketeer?' and I'll say, 'I am always a Mouseketeer.'" Reflecting on the influence of the show, she said, "Producers have a great responsibility when selling TV shows to children. They are molding those impressionable minds. Our show reported on current events, we had our own soap-opera series [the serials], we had musical variety and wonderful cartoons. Everybody does that today, but in different time slots. We had it all together — the best that TV had to offer kids."

"There weren't many role models for children in those days," stated Darlene. "The Mouseketeers were real people, just like the rest of the world. They even used their real names."

Tommy explained with much the same reasoning. "We were the kids next door. There was nothing phony about the show. There was nothing slick about the show. It was just kids having fun."

Cubby said he felt that the kids at home could tell the Mouseketeers were enjoying what they were doing. "We were having a great old time and I think it showed," he said. "We got to wear costumes and sing and dance, plus we were like family."

"I'm so grateful for 'The Mickey Mouse Club,'" said Annette. "I loved every minute of the experience. Some of the happiest years of my life were spent as a Mouseketeer."

"To me the show was just plain fun," Sharon said, with great enthusiasm. "But the best part of the experience was that the core group of kids were like family. We were raised in a kind of Fantasyland and got to be with each other every day, singing and dancing and going to school. Being a Mouseketeer follows you around your whole life. In a way, it's kind of a good-luck charm."

Sharon's mom, Nicki Baird, remarked of her daughter's tenure on "The Mickey Mouse Club": "Being at Disney Studio, working with other children, was wonderful. She wasn't treated as an adult, like some kids in show business are, she was treated as a kid. To me, that meant that Sharon could still keep her childhood."

Original "Mickey Mouse Club" publicist Leonard Shannon based the popularity of the show on the wealth of talent that contributed to the overall show. "I dare say that for the years the show was in production every available asset of Walt Disney Productions was put into service on the series. All the talent, all the creativity that the studio had to draw upon touched that show in one way or another." As for the Mouseketeers, Shannon remarked, "They worked because they were charming! And not only did they serve their purpose to entertain, but they were influential. They were significant."

So significant, that their influence propelled some kids to specific careers. "I began ballet lessons because I loved Annette Funicello," noted a fan. "In one episode, she tottered around en pointe in a white tutu. Now, because of that, I am a professional ballerina. Who would believe!"

"We ate, lived, and dreamed Disney Studio at that time," Tommy recalled. "If we weren't working at the studio, we were at Disneyland, and when we weren't there we were on tour. We were part of each other's lives and it was the greatest thing that could ever happen to me. People still come up and say, 'Thank you for my childhood,'

(Clockwise) Sherry, Sharon, Tommy, Don, Annette, and Bobby join today's contingent of Mouseketeers on the first anniversary of The Disney Channel's "Mickey Mouse Club" in 1990.

Sherry, Bobby, and Sharon during their appearance at the "First Disneyana Convention," held at Walt Disney World in 1992.

'Thank you for keeping me company,' 'Thank you for being who you are.' The core group of us, we were really a family. We socialized together, we played together, we got sick together and went through traumas together. We were a family of kids who really were like brothers and sisters. We had sibling rivalries and disagreements and we hugged each other and we celebrated birthdays. I believe the friendships we acquired with each other then are still deeply embedded in us."

According to Tommy, those close ties are sometimes most apparent onstage. "When we still perform, it's like we're tied by an umbilical cord. We know what the other person is thinking. We're feeling the other person's pain. We know when to make a move onstage because the other person is going to make it. We just do it automatically. It's part of us and that kinship is very special to me."

Amazingly, today the core group of Mouseketeers' lives are still interconnected. Bobby and Tommy's sons Robert and Casey go to the same school and are best friends. Lonnie's doctor is Sherry's husband, Dr. Richard Van Meter, and Tommy is still one of Lonnie's closest friends. Annette and Sharon speak on the phone every week and spend time together whenever Sharon (who lives in Reno, Nevada) visits Los Angeles. Birthday parties, anniversaries, and other special

God Bless "The Mickey Mouse Club."

occasions often bring them all together for group reunions. Even Mrs. Seaman, their studio schoolteacher, attended Sharon's fiftieth birthday party!

And, from a professional standpoint, it's still not over for the original Mouseketeers. In 1992, 1993, and 1994, a group of them appeared together again at the Disneyana Convention, a four-day symposium presented under the auspices of The Walt Disney Company, attended by Disney enthusiasts from around the world. Nineteen ninety-five will no doubt include many more surprises, since they will be celebrating their 40th anniversary on October 3rd.

In talking with me one day, Sharon Baird's positive Disney memories filled our conversation. But at one point she lamented, "There was an unhappy part of 'The Mickey Mouse Club.' The worst thing about it was that it ended."

If history is any indication, I can say with absolute conviction, "Cheer up, Sharon, I don't think so."

ORIGINAL MOUSEKETEERS
1955–59

Nancy Abbate	6/19/42	John Lee Johann	12/23/42
Don Agrati (Grady)	6/8/44	Bonni Lou Kern	1/2/41
Sherry Alberoni	12/2/46	Charley Laney	6/18/43
Sharon Baird	8/16/43	Larry Larsen	9/3/39
Billie Jean Beanblossom	1/1/44	Cubby O'Brien	7/14/46
Bobby Burgess	5/19/41	Karen Pendleton	7/1/46
Lonnie Burr	5/31/43	Paul Petersen	9/23/45
Tommy Cole	12/20/41	Lynn Ready	12/3/44
Johnny Crawford	3/26/46	Mickey Rooney, Jr.	unavailable
Dennis Day	7/12/42	Tim Rooney	unavailable
Eileen Diamond	6/15/43	Mary Lynn Sartori	1/4/43
Dickie Dodd	10/27/45	Bronson Scott	7/21/47
Mary Espinosa	1/16/45	Michael Smith (deceased)	8/29/45
Bonnie Lynn Fields	7/18/44	Jay-Jay Solari	9/12/43
Annette Funicello	10/22/42	Margene Storey	7/21/43
Darlene Gillespie	4/8/41	Ronnie Steiner	11/21/42
Judy Harriet	9/13/42	Mark Sutherland	12/17/44
Cheryl Holdridge	6/20/44	Doreen Tracey	4/3/43
Linda Hughes	10/22/46	Don Underhill	9/5/41
Dallas Johann	unavailable		

SELECTED LIST OF "MICKEY

Recordings (Disneyland Record Company)

The Musical Highlights from "The Mickey Mouse Club" TV Show
Twenty-seven New Songs from "The Mickey Mouse Club" TV Show
We're the Mouseketeers
Walt Disney's Song Fest (the Mouseketeers)
Songs for All the Holidays by the Mouseketeers
Songs from "The Mickey Mouse Club" Serials
"Annette" and Songs from Disney Serials
"Sleeping Beauty," by Darlene Gillespie

Publications and Comic Books

Mickey Mouse and the Missing Mouseketeers
Donald Duck and the Mouseketeers
Donald Duck Safety Book (MMC edition)
Donald Duck Prize Driver (MMC edition)
Donald Duck in Disneyland (MMC edition)
Little Man of Disneyland (MMC edition)
Davy Crockett's Keelboat Race (MMC edition)
Robin Hood (MMC edition)
Mother Goose (MMC edition)
Goofy Movie Star (MMC edition)
Mickey Mouse Flies the Christmas Mail (MMC edition)
Perri (MMC edition)
Peter and the Wolf (MMC edition)
Cinderella's Friends (MMC edition)
Bongo (MMC edition)
Corky and White Shadow
Spin and Marty (The Boys Who Rode for the Triple R)
Spin and Marty (Their Friendship Was Genuine, But...)
Spin and Marty and Annette — Pirates of Shell Island
Spin and Marty (Big Chief Whirlybird)
The Nature of Things
The Hardy Boys in Secret of the Old Mill
The Hardy Boys in Mystery of Ghost Farm
Clint and Mac
Jiminy Cricket
Mickey Mouse and Pluto Pup (MMC edition)
Mickey Mouse Stamp Book (MMC edition)
Mouseketeers Try Out Time

MOUSE CLUB" MERCHANDISE

"Mickey Mouse Club" Scrapbook (1st design)
"Mickey Mouse Club" Scrapbook (2nd design)

Coloring Books
Walt Disney's "Mickey Mouse Club" Box of 12 Books to Color
Mickey Mouse Coloring Book
"Mickey Mouse Club" Coloring Book (2 designs)
"Mickey Mouse Club" Coloring Book (3rd design)
"Mickey Mouse Club" Dot-to-Dot Coloring Book
"Mickey Mouse Club" Giant Funtime Coloring Book
Mousekartoon Coloring Book
Spin and Marty Coloring Book
Jimmie Dodd Coloring Book
Jimmie Dodd Magic Carpet Coloring Book
The Hardy Boys Coloring Book

Personalities: Annette, Linda, Mouseketeers
1956 Annette Cut-Out Doll Portfolio
1958 Annette Cut-Out Doll Portfolio
1960 Annette Cut-Out Doll Portfolio
1960 Annette Sierra Summer (Fiction)
1958 Annette — A Clue to the Mystery of the Missing Necklace (Comics)
1960 Annette's Life Story (Comics)
1961 Annette — Desert Inn Mystery (Fiction)
1961 Annette in Hawaii (Doll Portfolio)
1961 Annette Coloring Book
1962 Annette Coloring Book
1962 Annette — Mystery at Moonstone Bay (Fiction)
1962 Annette Boxed Paper Doll
1963 Annette Cut-Outs
1963 Annette Coloring Book
1963 Annette and The Mystery at Smugglers' Cove (Fiction)
1957 Mouseketeers Cut-Outs
1958 Linda Hughes Doll Portfolio
1961 Starlets (Doll Kit — 4 stand-up dolls with kits)
1963 Mouseketeers Cut-Outs

"MICKEY MOUSE CLUB" TV 1955–59 CREDITS

Although he requested that he not be listed in the on-screen TV credits, Walt Disney was indeed the overall producer and director of "The Mickey Mouse Club."

"MICKEY MOUSE CLUB" TV CREDITS 1955 THROUGH 1959

Order of names listed per Walt Disney Company History of "The Mickey Mouse Club"

Producer Bill Walsh

Associate Producers Mike Holoboff, Louis Debney, Tommy Walker, Malcolm Stuart Boylan

General Coordinators Mike Holoboff, Hal Adelquist, Chuck Dargan

Directors (including serials) Sidney Miller, Dik Darley, Jonathan Lucas, William Beaudine, Jr., Charles Haas, Larry Lansburgh, Charles Shows, Robert G. Shannon, R.G. Springsteen, Edward Sampson, Charles Barton, Bob Lehman, Fred Hartsook, Montie Montana, Charles Lamont, Hamilton S. Luske, Clyde Geronimi, Tommy Walker

Assistant Directors (including serials) Jack Cunningham, William Beaudine, Jr., Dolph Zimmer, Russ Haverick, Horace Hough, Erich von Stroheim, Jr., Vincent McEveety, Joseph L. McEveety, Tommy Foulkes, Les Gorall, Bill Finnegan, Les Philmer, Art Vitarelli, Gene Law

Cameramen (including serials) Gordon Avil, ASC, Edward Coleman, ASC, Walter H. Castle, ASC, John Martin, W.W. Goodpaster, Karl Maslowski, Herbert Knapp, Frederick Gately, Al Runkie, Duane R. Hoag, Lloyd Mason Smith, Tad Nichols, J. Carlos Carbajal, Charles P. Boyle, ASC, Arthur J. Ornitz

Film Editors Cotton Warburton, ACE, Al Teeter, Joseph S. Dietrick, George Nicholson, John O. Young, Lee Huntington, Robert Stafford, George Gale, ACE, Jack Vandagriff, Ed Sampson, Jim Love, Wayne Hughes, Laurie Vejar, Edward R. Baker, Lloyd Richardson, Hugh Chaloupka, Jr., Ernest Palmer, Carlos Savage, Ellsworth Hoagland, ACE, Anthony Gerard, Stanley Johnson, ACE, Bill Lewis, Paul Capon

Special Processes Ub Iwerks, ASC, Eustace Lycett

Music Buddy Baker, Franklyn Marks, Joseph S. Dubin, William Lava, Joseph Mullendore, Paul Smith, Oliver Wallace, Herman D. Koppel, Clifford Vaughn, Frank Worth, Richard Aurandt, Jaime Mendoza Nava, Temple Abady, Edward Plumb

Songs Jimmie Dodd, Gil George, Charlie Shows, Tom Adair, Larry Orenstein, Bob Amsberry, Ruth Carroll, Stan Jones, Larry Adelson, Roy Williams, Martin Schwab, Imogene Carpenter, Oliver Wallace, Cliff Edwards, Franklyn Marks, Sam Sykens, Bob Russell, Ray Darby, George Bruns, Jack Spiers, Paul Smith, Muzzy Marceleno, Erdman Penner, Larry Morey, Eliot Daniel, Frances Jeffords, Sidney Fine, Ron Salt, Jeanne Gayle, Ed Penner, Mack David, Al Hoffman, Jerry Livingston, Marvin Ash, Ray Brenne, Bob Russell, Carl Sigman, Bob Jackman, Fess Parker, Buddy Ebsen

Conductor Leo Damiani (Burbank Symphony)

Sound Robert O. Cook, Sid A. Manor

Re-recording Editor Reese Overacker

Choreography Tom Mahoney, Burch Holtzman (Burch Mann)

Art Directors Bruce Bushman, Marvin Aubrey Davis, Carroll Clark

Set Decoration Bertram Granger, Fred Maclean, Emil Kuri, William L. Stevens, Vin Taylor, Armor E. Goetten

Costumes Chuck Keehne

Makeup Pat McNalley, Tom Bartholomew, David Newell, Joe Hadley

Facilities Coordinator Ben Harris

Production Managers Ben Chapman, Mike Holoboff, Douglas Peirce

Production Supervisors Mike Holoboff, Lou Debney, Perce Pearce, Alan L. Jaggs, Stirling Silliphant, Bill Park, Hal Ramser, Charles Shows, Ben Sharpsteen, Harry Tytle, Jack Cutting, Gene Armstrong, Larry Clemmons

Writers Lillie Hayward, Lee Chaney, Bill Cox, Jackson Gillis, Charles Shows, John and Rosalie Bodrero, Astrid Henning, Charles Haas, Larry Clemmons, Janet Lansburgh

"MICKEY MOUSE CLUB" MOUSEKETEERS
1977 SERIES

Scott Craig
Nita "Dee" Di Giampaolo
Mindy Feldman
Angel Florez

Allison Fonte
Shawnte Northcutte
Kelly Parsons
Julie Piekarski

Todd Turquand
Lisa Whelchel
Curtis Wong

"MICKEY MOUSE CLUB" MOUSEKETEERS
THE DISNEY CHANNEL

Ackerman, Josh
Aguilera, Christina
Alley, Lindsey
Bennett, Rhona
Booth, Nita
Brooks, Mylin
Brown, Brandy
Carson, Blain
Chasez, J. C.
Danner, Braden
Danner, Tasha
DeLoach, Nikki
Fantini, T. J.

Fields, Albert
Godboldo, Dale
Gosling, Ryan
Hale, Tiffini
Hampton, Chase
Herring, Roqué
Kater, David
Lucca, Tony
Luna, Ricky
Lynche, Tate
McGill, Jennifer
McNair, Terra
Magno, Deedee

Miller, Ilana
Minor, Jason
Misner, Terri (adult)
Morris, Matt
Newman, Fred (adult)
Osgood, Kevin
Pampolina, Damon
Pryor, Mowava (adult)
Russell, Keri
Spears, Britney
Timberlake, Justin
Worden, Marc

THE DISNEY CHANNEL
"MICKEY MOUSE CLUB" FACT SHEET

WHAT: "Mickey Mouse Club" — a half-hour series taped before a live studio audience

WHERE: The Disney/MGM Studios in Lake Buena Vista, Florida

WHEN: The show debuted in April 1989 and currently airs Monday through Friday 5:30-6 p.m. (ET/PT) on The Disney Channel.

CONCEPT: "Mickey Mouse Club" features 20 talented young people, ages 11 to 18, from across North America. The after-school club features music, dance, celebrity guests, comedy skits, and informative segments about issues affecting teens today.

ELEMENTS: Various theme days are featured throughout the week:

"Music Day" is when such performers as Jeremy Jordan, Brian McKnight, Boy Krazy, Shai, and SWV entertain.

"Guest Day" is when club members at home get to spend the day with such personalities as Brian Austin Green ("Beverly Hills 90210"), Jenna Von Oy ("Blossom"), and the "Home Improvement" boys, Zachery Ty Bryan, Taran Smith, and Jonathan Taylor Thomas, either at home, at work, or participating in their favorite activities.

"Hall of Fame Day" is when young people from around the country are recognized for outstanding achievements and inducted into "The Mickey Mouse Club" Hall of Fame.

"Party Day" is when the Mouseketeers celebrate with special themes each week.

"What I Wanna Be/See" is a weekly segment that provides viewers the opportunity to explore a wide range of career choices and travel to places they have never seen.

BIBLIOGRAPHY

Keller, Keith. *The Mickey Mouse Club Scrapbook.* Grosset & Dunlap, 1975.

Lasky, Betty. *RKO. The Biggest Little Major of Them All.* Roundtable, 1989.

Munsey, Cecil. *Disneyana: Walt Disney Collectibles.* Hawthorn Books,Inc., 1974.

Petersen, Paul. *Walt, Mickey and Me.* Dell Books, 1977.

Thomas, Bob. *Walt Disney, An American Original.* Hyperion, 1994 (originally published by Simon & Schuster, 1976).

Woolery, George W. *Children's Television: The First Thirty-Five Years.* Scarecrow, 1985.

Walt Disney: Famous Quotes. Disney's Kingdom Editions, 1994.

Walt Disney's Mickey Mouse Club Magazine, vol. I, no. 1, Winter, 1956.

INDEX

Page numbers in *italics* refer to captions